Hooking HIM

Shooting Stars Series

Fighting to Breathe
Wide Open Spaces
One Last Wish

Fluke My Life Series

Running into Love
Stumbling into Love
Tossed into Love
Drawn into Love

How to Catch an Alpha Series

Catching Him
Baiting Him

Ruby Falls Series

Falling Fast

Written as C. A Rose

Alfha Law Series

Justified
Liability
Verdict

Stand-Alone Title

Finders Keepers

Hooking HIM

Aurora Rose Reynolds

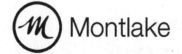
Montlake

Published by Montlake, Seattle
www.apub.com

Amazon, the Amazon logo, and Montlake are trademarks of Amazon.com, Inc., or its affiliates.

ISBN-13: 9781542014533
ISBN-10: 1542014530

Cover design by Letitia Hasser

Printed in the United States of America

This isn't a dedication; it's a suggestion:
Live every single day of your life like it's your last.
Drink when you want, laugh until your soul is full,
open yourself up to falling in love, spend time with
people who are important, and enjoy every moment,
even the scary ones.

Suggestion 1

FIRST IMPRESSIONS ARE EVERYTHING.

DIDN'T YOUR MAMA TEACH YOU THAT?

ANNA

"Are you happy?" my friend Lucy asks, and I instinctively tighten my fingers around my cell phone as I put my bare feet up on the wooden rail in front of me. I've lived most of my life in the city, surrounded by skyscrapers and the constant sound of chatter and traffic, with air clogged with the scents of food and exhaust. Now, sitting on the back deck of my studio apartment in a small coastal town in South Carolina, with the ocean mere feet away, the sun warming my skin, and a slight breeze playing in my hair, I wonder how I survived in Chicago for so long.

"I'm getting there," I answer, smiling as I watch a young family laughing and playing in the surf nearby.

"Even living in a small studio apartment and working at a bakery?" She sounds skeptical, and I remind myself she just doesn't understand. Like everyone else back in Chicago, she doesn't get why I'd choose to go from making over $60,000 a year, living in a beautiful penthouse apartment, planning a wedding to a good man—who also happens to be gorgeous—to moving to a town where I know almost no one. Where I'm renting an apartment the size of my old bathroom and working a job that pays in a month what I used to make in a week.

"Even living in an apartment and working at the bakery," I reply, keeping my tone neutral before adding quietly, "I do miss you, though." It's not a lie: Lucy has been in my life since I can remember. Our parents were friends, so we practically grew up together.

"I still don't get it," she says with a sigh, and my heart sinks. I keep hoping she will, but as the months pass, it's becoming more and more clear that she won't. None of my friends or family do. They don't understand that I didn't just wake up one day and decide to give everything up. Every day for years, I woke up and looked at myself in the mirror, disliking the materialistic, shallow woman I was becoming. Until one day I decided to do something about it.

"I should let you go. I'm sure you have stuff to do, and I promised Edie that I'd go with her to bingo."

"Bingo? You're playing bingo?" She laughs.

I can't help the smile that tips up my lips. "Yeah, it's actually kind of fun."

"If you say so," she says, sounding distracted, and then a moment later, a distinctive male voice in the background asks her something, and I know it's Lance, my ex-fiancé, who's a partner at her firm. "Sorry, I gotta go, Anna."

"No problem," I tell her, feeling nauseous. "Bye." I hang up before she has a chance to reply and then sit forward, dropping my head into my hands as I think back to the look on Lance's face when I gave him back his ring and told him that we were over. He didn't say a word and walked away, looking devastated. The hardest part about leaving Chicago wasn't the lifestyle I was giving up; it was losing him. Even though I wasn't in love with him, he was my friend. For the five years we were in a relationship, he was a constant in my life, someone I depended on for support, and he was one of the few people who understood the dysfunctional relationship I had with my parents and encouraged me to take a step back from them when they hurt me with their carelessness.

Not wanting to spend the day dwelling on something that would leave me depressed, I pull in a deep breath, expecting to inhale the fresh sea air, but my nose wrinkles when the distinct scent of pot hits me. I open my eyes, get up from my lounger, and stop midway across the deck when a big puff of smoke floats up from the porch below. I walk quietly to the edge and look over the rail, wondering if someone from the beach has decided to hide out and get high. But then I shake my head when I see Dixie and Pearl, my landlady Edie's best friends, who are in their seventies, standing at her back door and sharing what looks like a joint: an object that seems out of place, given their grandmotherly appearance. Both women are dressed like they're about to go golfing, in their pastel polo shirts and khaki capris, all capped by white hair that's styled, like always, in an array of curls.

"Isn't weed illegal?"

Both women jump, and Dixie, who's holding the joint, tosses it away, yelling "Oh shit!" while Pearl screams, searching until she finds me on the deck above.

"Anna!" Pearl says, glaring. "You scared the dickens out of me."

"Dickens," Dixie says with a giggle as the back door opens.

"What on earth is going on out here?" Edie asks, stepping outside wearing a white linen outfit with her short hair feathered back from a gracefully aging face.

"Anna tried to give us heart attacks," Pearl says accusingly, pointing up at me, and Edie tips her head back, smiling when she spots me.

Edie was the first person I met when I moved to South Carolina. She had an apartment for rent in her house, and when I answered the ad, she invited me over to view the space. I fell in love with it because it was right on the beach, but after spending an hour with her, I also wanted the apartment because it would give me an excuse to spend time with her. I didn't understand why I was so drawn to her at first, but something about being in her presence made me feel hopeful. Then one night, over wine, she opened up about her past and told me about her ex-husband, who she was with for more than twenty years before she found the courage to leave him. And when she did, she found a way to be happy, even when he and her family were all sure she would come back with her tail tucked between her legs. I guess her story gave me the hope to fight for my own happiness.

"They're smoking weed," I inform her, waving my hand at both women.

"I have glaucoma." Pearl plants her hands on her hips.

"Really?" I ask, and her eyes narrow on mine in challenge.

"It's time for us to go anyway," Edie announces.

"Found it!" Dixie shouts, and Pearl breaks her stare-down with me to turn to her friend, who holds up the joint like it's a trophy.

"Anna." My eyes move to Edie. "Meet us at the car. I want to get to the bingo hall before Carol so she doesn't take our table."

"That woman is annoying," Dixie mutters.

"She's such a show-off," Pearl says, taking the joint from Dixie and wrapping what's left of it in a tissue she pulls from her bra. "Who cares that you have five grandkids when they don't even like you?"

"Right!" Dixie agrees while opening the door for Pearl to go inside before her.

"Meet us in the driveway," Edie says, and I narrow my eyes on hers. "What?"

"I notice you're not saying anything about them smoking pot. Did you smoke with them?"

"Not today." She winks, then disappears inside. I watch the door close behind her, unsure if she's joking. She, Pearl, and Dixie might all be older than me, but you'd never know by the way they act and the things they say.

"Well, today should be interesting," I sigh to myself before going into my apartment and shutting the door. I walk between my bed and the open kitchen to the closet and slide my feet into a pair of flip-flops before grabbing a plaid button-down shirt and tying it around my waist. I learned the first time Edie dragged me to the bingo hall that they keep the room a degree above freezing—something that wouldn't have been bad if I hadn't dressed for the heat and humidity outside. I stop and grab my keys, along with my purse, then lock up before taking the stairs down to the driveway, where Edie, Dixie, and Pearl are waiting.

"I can drive." I hold up the keys to my Ford, and they all turn in my direction.

"Where's the rest of your shorts?" Pearl asks, and I look down at my denim cutoffs, which are short but not any shorter than what girls wear nowadays. Still, they're shorter than anything I would've worn a year ago.

"Oh, stop. If you had legs like hers, you'd show them off too," Edie scolds, and I glance up, catching her shaking her head at her friend before she looks at me. "Anna, you drive like an old lady. You're riding shotgun. Get in." She presses a button on her keys, and the doors unlock.

"I don't drive like an old lady," I say to defend myself as I open the door to her red BMW convertible and pull the seat forward for Pearl and Dixie to get in the back.

"The last time I rode with you, you drove thirty in a fifty."

"It was a construction zone. I was following the rules."

"It was after eight at night. They weren't even working."

"Whatever." I push the seat back into place and get in. I reach for my seat belt as she starts the engine and lowers the roof. As soon as the top locks into place, she backs out of the driveway, and I'm reaching out for the handle on the door when I hear her laugh.

"Relax, child. I've never gotten in an accident."

"Really?" I glance at her quickly, not wanting to take my eyes off the road, even though I'm not the one driving.

"Well . . . maybe I should say I have never gotten into an accident that was my fault."

"That sounds a little more believable," I reply, then pull in a sharp breath as she turns onto the on-ramp for the highway and presses her foot more firmly on the gas. I hold my breath as she merges into traffic and then squeeze my eyes closed as she zooms forward to pass in front of a semi. I feel the car start to slow and open my eyes. I release the breath I've been holding as we take the next exit and stop at a red light. When the light turns green, my fingers tighten on the handle of the door, turning my knuckles white as she takes a right and presses the gas once more. I start to pray when she hugs the bumper of the car in front of us, and then my heart drops into my stomach when I hear the distinctive sound of police sirens.

"Oh shit," comes from the back seat as Edie pulls over and places the car in park. I look over my shoulder and watch Pearl reach into her shirt, pull out a white tissue, and shove it under the seat in front of her.

Oh my God. "Was that your joint?" I shout, and Pearl glares at me.

"Just be cool. This isn't a big deal." Edie wraps her hand around my upper leg, and I focus on her and nod, not feeling cool at all. My leg starts to bounce as we wait for the officer to get out of his car, and by the time he gets to Edie's window, it's jumping like crazy.

"Edie."

A deep voice greets us, and I turn my head, noticing first the long, masculine fingers wrapped around the top of the door, then dark jeans, a black belt with a badge attached, and a formfitting blue button-down that's tucked in, making it clear the guy is fit. I slowly lift my head as I take in his broad shoulders, and my heart starts to pound for a different reason when I reach his face. Holy wow, even with his eyes covered with a pair of silver aviators that look amazing on him, he's still heart-stoppingly gorgeous. I stare at him, unsure if it's his dark hair, sharp jaw, or full lips that have me entranced. All I know is it's a good thing he has those glasses on. I don't think I could handle seeing all of him at one time.

"Calvin, how's your mom?" Pearl asks sweetly from the back seat, and he turns his head just slightly to look at her while I keep my eyes on him. Calvin—that name fits him. It makes me think of those old Calvin Klein ads with Marky Mark that my friends and I used to drool over.

"She's good."

"Tell her I say hello."

"Will do." He dips his chin before shifting his attention back to Edie. "Do you know why I pulled you over?"

"I have no idea," Edie says. Then she asks, "Was I speeding?"

"You weren't speeding. But I followed you onto the highway and off, and I'm a little concerned with your lack of turn signals and the way you tend to test the boundaries of your brakes when driving behind someone."

"My car has great brakes," she informs him with a smile.

"That might be, but I doubt you'd feel that way if the person you followed so closely had to hit their brakes and you, in turn, hit them."

"You're absolutely right." She places her hand on her chest, looking surprised. "I never thought of that."

"I'm sure." His jaw tics, making my fingers, still on the handle, clench. "If I see you driving like that again, Edie, I'll give you a ticket. And you and I both know you can't have any more points on your license."

Points? She already has points on her license?

"How many tickets have you gotten?" I blurt, and all eyes rest on me, including a pair covered with a silver tint.

"I still have my license," Edie tells me.

"One more ticket and you won't," Calvin adds.

"One more ticket" meaning she's gotten a few? "I knew I should have ignored my need to respect my elders and demanded to drive. First, Pearl and Dixie smoking a—"

"Pardon?" Calvin rumbles, cutting off the word *joint*, and my eyes widen. Oh crap. My mouth goes dry. I wave my hand in his direction and shake my head once more. "They were smoking a cigarette. Even at their age, they should know those things kill." I can't see his eyes, but I still feel them bore into mine. I shift in my seat but try to keep my expression neutral. "I'll make sure Edie's more careful when she's behind the wheel."

He acknowledges my statement with a grunt and comes out of his bent position, which forces me to tip my head back. "This is your last warning." He taps Edie's door before he walks back toward his car. I turn to watch him, thinking even from behind, his broad shoulders and slim waist are attractive.

"I can't believe you were going to tell him that we were smoking a joint," Pearl hisses.

"She didn't and she covered for us," Dixie mutters. "I don't blame her for getting weird. He's handsome, and that happens when you're talking to a handsome man."

"Do you think he's handsome?" Edie asks me, and I look over at her, noting a calculating look in her eyes.

Damn.

"Of course she thinks he's attractive. She's female," Pearl says from the back seat.

"Well?" Edie asks.

"Um . . ." I shift under her stare. "He's okay."

"Okay?" Dixie snorts. "That man is not just okay, darling, and if you think that, you need to be checked by a doctor to confirm you actually have a pulse."

"Whatever. Shouldn't we go? Aren't you the one who didn't want to be late to bingo?"

"Fine, you win this one," Edie says after a long moment, and then she puts the shifter in drive, flips on her turn signal, and checks her mirror. The moment she starts to pull away from the side of the road and into traffic, the car is jolted to the right, and the sounds of metal crunching and scraping fill the air.

With wide eyes and my heart pounding, I turn and meet a pair of mesmerizing blue eyes belonging to Calvin. Holy cow, we just sideswiped a cop! I drag my eyes off his and focus on Edie. "Are you okay?"

"I'm fine. Are you?" Her eyes scan me from head to toe.

"I'm good." I look over my shoulder and see Calvin backing up behind us, then look at the two wide-eyed women in the back seat. "Are you two all right?"

"I'm okay," Pearl says shakily.

"Just a little shook up, but I'm okay," Dixie replies.

"I'm going to make sure Calvin is all right." I unhook my belt and open my door.

With my legs shaking, I walk around the back of the car, but I stop short when I see Calvin bent over and looking in the open trunk of his cruiser. Without even a glance in my direction, he booms, "Get back into the vehicle."

"But—"

"Back in the vehicle." He doesn't move except to turn his head, and his eyes come to me. "It's not safe for you to be out here."

"I just wanted to make sure you were okay," I tell him, and he comes out of his bent position and walks toward me slowly.

I should back away. I want to back away, but I hold my ground until he reaches out and wraps his hand around my upper arm.

"What are you doing?" I look at where he's holding me and automatically try to tug free, but he doesn't let go. Instead, he starts walking, forcing me to go with him. When we reach the passenger side of the car, he opens the door and urges me to sit.

"Stay," he orders, and I blink up at him in disbelief.

"I'm not a dog you can just order to do something," I hiss, tucking my feet into the car.

"Yeah, I know. My dog actually listens." He slams the door and walks away, leaving me fuming.

CALVIN

I shut down my computer and lean back in my chair, rubbing my eyes. It's been a long day, a long month, and an even longer year. I need a vacation, preferably near a lake where I can spend my days drinking beer, fishing, and watching the sun set while doing both those things.

With a weary sigh, I roll my chair back and start to get up when my cell phone rings. When I see my mother's name on the screen, I sigh for a completely different reason. Without answering, I know she's calling about what went down with the Golden Girls and their newest recruit, Anna. Anna Belle McAlister, a woman with hair that reminds me of warm whiskey, eyes the color of an evergreen forest, and skin that looks kissed by the sun. Not a beautiful woman—a gorgeous one who's had me thinking of sweaty nights wrapped in cotton sheets all damned day.

Fuck.

I grab my phone, swipe my finger across the screen, and place it against my ear. "Mom."

"Calvin, I just got off the telephone with Pearl a moment ago, and I . . . I just . . . good Lord, Calvin. Did you honestly speak to a woman like she was Bane, then go on to tell her that Bane is better behaved than she is because he listens?"

I knew it.

"Mom, I told you before you need to stop listening to that woman and her posse."

"So you didn't say those things?"

I tip my head back toward the ceiling and shake my head. "The woman you're referring to was just in a car accident. I asked her to go back to the car to get out of harm's way. When she didn't listen, I escorted her to the vehicle."

"And then?" she asks.

"And then I contained the scene of the accident and did my job."

"You're leaving out the part about when you talked to a woman—who, from what Pearl says, is sweet—like she was a dog." I listen to her let out a deep breath. "Boy, you do my head in."

"So you've been saying since I can remember."

"I know I raised you better than that, Calvin Miller. And I'm telling you now that you need to apologize to that girl."

"Mom, I'm not going to apologize for doing my job."

"No, you're going to apologize for being rude to her."

"I'll get right on that."

"I'm serious, Calvin Drake Miller. You better apologize." She doesn't shout, but I still know she's serious by the tone of her voice.

"Fine. Are we done?" I stand and pick up my badge, clipping it back on my belt, then grab my keys.

"Yes. Now, are you still coming over for dinner tomorrow?"

"I'll be there," I agree as I walk out to the main room of the station, lifting my chin to a few other officers as I pass them on my way toward the exit.

"Good. I'll see you at six. Maybe you can invite Anna. That's her name, by the way. Pearl said she just moved to town and is working at the Sweet Spot. Maybe you can stop by there tomorrow and invite her to dinner."

"I'm not inviting her to dinner."

"Why on earth not?"

"I'll see you tomorrow," I say, ignoring her question.

"Invite her to dinner."

"I gotta go, Mom."

"Fine, love you. Talk to you tomorrow." She hangs up, and I shove my phone into my back pocket, then walk out of the building toward my truck, parked on the street. I get in, start the engine, and head through town.

When I reach my place, I get out and head through the gate and up the front walk. I hear Bane bark as I get close to the front door. The barking stops as I put my key in the lock, and then, just like always when I arrive home, Bane greets me, circling my feet as I shut the door and then flip on the light.

"Hey, boy." I rub the top of his head and sit to take off my boots. I then give him a rubdown before I get up and head for the kitchen. I go to the pantry for his food and fill his bowl, then walk to the fridge, grab a beer, and then take a gulp before looking for something to heat up for dinner. And like I've done every night for the last five years, ever since the woman I thought I was going to marry walked away because she was unable to handle my career as a police officer, I eat while watching TV, then go to bed alone, with only my dog to keep me company. But for the first time in five years, I wonder if it's fucking time to put myself out there again.

Suggestion 2

SAY NO, EVEN IF YOU WANT TO SAY YES

ANNA

"You know if Gaston comes in and sees what you're doing, he will lose his mind, right?" I ask Chrissie—my boss, the owner of the Sweet Spot, and a woman I now consider a friend.

"What Gus doesn't know won't hurt him." She grins, and I look at her stomach, which has grown considerably over the last few months, and the large bag of flour she's dumping into one of the plastic storage containers.

I walk to her and take the bag, ignoring her grumbling as I take over. "I'm pretty sure he's installed cameras in here just to make sure you're not overdoing it." It's a joke, but in all honesty, I wouldn't put it past him to have done something like that. He's very protective of his wife, and his protective nature only seems to have grown since she got pregnant.

"I would kill him," she says, looking around like she's searching for a hidden camera. I smile, then glance at her when she asks, "How was your day off yesterday?"

"Good—just a normal day, except I went to go play bingo with Edie, and on the way, she got pulled over, then accidentally hit the cop who pulled her over."

"What?" Her eyes widen.

I set the bag of flour down and lean against the counter. "It was a mess. She checked her side mirror but not the blind spot, so she didn't see that he had pulled out until she'd sideswiped him, and by then it was too late. Now she has to go in front of a judge to see if she should still be allowed to drive."

"I've heard rumors she's a menace on the road."

"I'm not sure those are rumors. Still, I hope things work out. It's going to be difficult for her if her license is taken away."

"I bet." She shakes her head. "She's always been independent, so I'm sure even the idea of her losing her license is not something she wants to consider."

"Yeah," I agree. "But I told her that if it does happen, I'll drive her around, and Pearl and Dixie both said the same, so it's not like she'll be stuck at home all the time." I pick up the bag of flour and carry it to the storage bins before dropping it inside one. "Anyway," I say, walking back toward her, "I had a chance to look over the applications you left on the desk in the office, and there were a few really good candidates. I was thinking maybe we should each pick our favorite from the bunch and bring them in for a second interview."

"That's a great idea. Gus wants me to have at least two people hired and trained as soon as possible. That way you'll have the help you need when I do go into labor and after the baby is born."

I glance down at her stomach as she starts to rub it and know we don't have long. She's already at seven months, and if she's anything like a few of my girlfriends in Chicago who've had kids, she's not going to feel like working the last few weeks of pregnancy. "I think even if we find one really good person to hire full time, I'll be okay while you're out for a few months."

"I know you'll be okay, but I also want you to be able to have two days off a week to play bingo or . . . I don't know, go on a date or two." She shrugs while shooting me a look I've found her giving me more and more often. A look that states she wants me to have a life outside of her shop and to meet a man. Something that is actually funny because she's told me herself that she wasn't looking for a man when she met her now husband; things between them just kind of happened.

That said, I do need a life, but I do not need to date. I spent five years with Lance and was in the middle of planning our wedding when I realized I wasn't just going to be hurting myself by marrying him; I would eventually end up hurting him, too, and he didn't deserve that.

Regardless of the fact that I wasn't in love with him, I cared about him deeply. Our relationship was comfortable, and our plans for our future were predictable. He checked every box my parents wanted. He was well educated, came from a good family, and was wealthy. My parents always had grand dreams of me being a trophy wife. When other little girls were told to study and do well in school so they might someday become a doctor or a lawyer, my parents told me to watch my figure, dress appropriately, and look for a man who would be able to give me a good life.

I did what they wanted. I met Lance when I was twenty-two while working at his family's company as the secretary to the CEO. I hated that job, but it paid really well, and in my parents' eyes, it was respectable. Or I should say it was something they were okay with me doing until I got married and had babies, who I would spend the rest of my life raising while doing the occasional charity event. After we got engaged, I thought, *Finally, finally my parents are happy, so maybe I'll be happy too.* But as the months turned into years, I realized it would never happen: not if I was living for them in an attempt to get them to love me. That's why, when I made the choice to leave my life in Chicago, I promised myself I wouldn't date again until I was happy with myself and my life.

"Earth to Anna." I blink, coming out of my thoughts as Chrissie snaps her fingers in front of my face.

"Sorry. I spaced for a second."

"I see that. Are you okay?" she asks, studying me closely.

"Yeah, fine." I wave her off. "I didn't sleep much last night." It's not a lie. I spent way too long on my balcony, watching the tide come in and the stars brighten the sky—something I don't take for granted. I never got to experience the night sky when I lived in the city. I mean, yes, there were stars, but I never took the time to actually enjoy them, and the night sky there can't compare to here.

"Did you fall asleep outside again?" she asks with a grin.

"No." I roll my eyes. "And that only happened one time."

"I know, but it's still funny when I think about you waking up to Edie, Dixie, and Pearl skinny-dipping."

"You think it's funny. I beg to differ," I say, but I still can't stop myself from laughing at the memory of waking up and seeing them running out into the surf in the nude.

"Those three are crazy."

"They are, but I kind of love how they devour life, even at their age."

"True," she agrees with a thoughtful look. "So about you dating. I think I might know someone—"

"No." I cut her off, then soften my tone, not wanting to hurt her feelings. "I'm not ready."

She reaches out, grasping my hand. "Anna."

"I will date . . ." I cover her hand with mine. "One day. Just not yet." Her expression softens; then we both look toward the doorway that leads to the front of the shop when the chime dings, letting us know someone has come in. "It's not Gaston. He would already be shouting for you," I say, and she giggles, squeezing my hand before letting it go, and I focus on her.

"Do you mind getting that? I'm going to go place the order for next week."

"No problem. Also, make sure you add extra lemons to the list. I want to make lemon bars again. They were a hit last weekend."

"Got it." She winks, then starts toward the office as I head out to the front of the shop.

When I clear the doorway, I frown when I don't see anyone. Then every single cell in my body seems to freeze when an all-too-familiar man rises out of a squat from in front of the display case.

"You." The word comes out in a whisper.

"Anna." Calvin's deep voice washes across my skin, making me tingle in a few unwanted places.

"What are you doing here?" I ask, wondering how he knows my name. The last time I saw him, he was leaving in his police cruiser after issuing Edie a ticket, along with informing her that she wasn't allowed to drive, so she'd have to find someone else to take the wheel.

All without even sparing me a glance.

"I wanted to apologize for yesterday."

"You're forgiven," I say instantly.

He tips his head to the side, and I don't want to find that subtle movement attractive, but I can't help myself. Dammit. "What exactly are you forgiving me for?"

"Whatever you're apologizing for."

He grins, and damn if that isn't attractive too. "Well, since that's done, what do you recommend?"

I shake my head, and my brows draw together. "What?"

"What do you recommend?"

"Do you mean from here?" I wave my hands around the shop.

He looks around, then asks somewhat sarcastically, "Isn't this a bakery?"

My right cheek twitches, a tic that surfaces when I'm feeling annoyed or uncomfortable. "No, it's actually a cover for a money-laundering operation. The stuff in the display case isn't even real. It's all made from plastic." I slip my most wide-eyed, innocent look into place. "Pretty amazing, right?"

He bites his bottom lip like he's trying not to laugh, and I have the urge to go over-the-top, Christian Grey alpha on his ass and demand he not do that. "Gorgeous . . . and a smart-ass."

Wait. Is he saying I'm gorgeous?

Never mind. I don't care. Time to get us back on track. "Everything here is good."

"Everything." He eyes me in a way that causes my nipples to pebble against the lace of my bra.

I cross my arms over my chest to hide the evidence that my body finds him attractive and hitch out my hip. "I'm sure if you live in town you've heard that this is the best place to take care of whatever sweet craving you might have."

"I haven't heard that, but I'm thinking you might be right."

I start to open my mouth to ask him what exactly he's doing here when the door chimes. It's Chrissie's husband, Gaston, looking as handsome as ever, even dressed casually in sneakers, jeans, and a plain navy-blue shirt. I would have sworn Gaston was the most attractive man in town, and Chrissie's best friend's husband, Tyler, second to him. But now, after meeting Calvin, I know I was wrong.

"Hey, Anna." He smiles at me before scanning the bakery. "Is Chrissie in the back?"

"Yeah, she's in the office, placing the order for next week."

He nods, then eyes Calvin at the counter. He lifts his chin at him before asking me, "Are you good?"

"Yep, this is Officer Miller." I wave one hand out in Calvin's direction.

"Detective," Calvin says.

"Okay, this is *Detective* Miller," I say, emphasizing the word sarcastically. "He came in today to make sure we're on the up-and-up."

"What?" Gus frowns, turning his attention to Calvin. "Is there a problem?"

"Nope, Anna here was just telling me about the shop being a cover for a money-laundering operation, which surprised me, since it's never come up on our radar."

Me and my big mouth.

"Anna." I turn to Gaston when he calls my name and wait for him to say more, but he doesn't. Instead, he looks between Calvin and me a couple of times, and then his expression fills with some sort of understanding that I do not get, and he shakes his head. "I'm going to go check on Chrissie and see if she has time to go get lunch."

"Okay," I say, and he glances at us once more before muttering something under his breath and disappearing into the back of the shop. Once he's gone, I turn to Calvin. "I swear if you get me fired, I will kill you."

"Are you threatening an officer?" he asks, his right brow rising slightly.

"What?"

"You just threatened a police officer."

"No." I shake my head, then point at him. "*I* just threatened *you*, a man who spoke to me like I was a dog."

"You already forgave me for that." He grins and crosses his arms over his broad chest. "You can't bring it up again."

"I can do whatever I want." Seriously, why does this guy make me want to scream and stomp my foot like a child who was told she can't get what she wants from the candy aisle in the grocery store?

"So it's true what they say about redheads." His eyes drift over my hair, then my face.

Knowing exactly what he means, I lean slightly toward him. "You have no idea. So maybe you should take that into consideration before coming in here again."

"Are you always crazy, or is it just me who brings out that quality in you?"

"I'm not crazy," I deny, and he grins. "And don't smile like that," I demand, and he bites his bottom lip once more. "And don't do that either. It's annoying."

"What is?"

"The whole lip-biting thing. It's annoying. Stop doing it," I demand, stomping my foot for emphasis.

"Stop being cute."

"I'm not being cute," I growl. Then I hiss, "Now tell me what you want, or leave."

"Are you an option?"

"No."

He smirks, then drops his gaze to the display case. "I'll take three of the maple bars and one of the double chocolate chip brownies." I grab a paper bag and quickly place each of the items inside. After folding over the top, I close it with the sticker I designed, of a cupcake with THE SWEET SPOT swirled into the pink-and-blue icing.

I place it on the counter in front of him, then ring up the purchase, pressing the buttons harder than necessary. "That will be twelve thirty-nine." I tap my foot as he swipes his credit card, and once the transaction is approved, I wait for him to leave, but he doesn't. Instead, he opens the bag, pulls out one of the maple bars, and takes a bite. I shouldn't find him eating attractive, but there is something about the way his full lips and strong jaw look as he bites and chews that makes me want to lean across the counter to kiss him.

Damn, damn, damn.

"So tell me, Anna," he says after swallowing. "Are you seeing anyone?"

"That is none of your business," I say, enunciating each word.

"She's not seeing anyone."

I turn quickly to glare at Chrissie, who's just appeared and is smiling widely, and then I transfer my glare to Gaston when he chuckles.

"Thanks," Calvin says, and I hear humor in that one word. I turn to face him, keeping my glare in place.

"Aren't you leaving?" I wave a hand toward the door.

"You're not making me feel very welcome."

"Because you're not," I bite out in frustration. I know I should be nice, especially with my boss standing feet away, but I don't like that I'm attracted to him, and I really don't like that I like the idea of him being attracted to me.

"Go out with me."

"No."

He casually shrugs one shoulder, then places the rest of the maple bar back into the bag and closes it. "All right. I'll see you around."

I don't miss the warning, and my pulse skips when his eyes lock with mine and he licks his index finger, then his thumb. I try to think of something to say, but my brain seems to have short-circuited.

"Later, Anna," he says to me; then he lifts his chin toward Chrissie and Gaston before he turns and walks away without another word. I stare at the door as he disappears through it, wondering what the heck I've just gotten myself into.

"Good Lord," Chrissie breathes. "That man is seriously hot, and that whole licking thing . . ." I turn to catch her shaking her head. "I don't even have words for what that was."

"I'm standing right here," Gaston says, glaring at his wife.

"I know." She looks up at him, placing her hand on his chest, and his expression softens. "I'm just stating the obvious." She turns her head to catch my eye. "Are you seriously not interested in going out with him?"

"I'm seriously not interested in going out with him," I lie. I'm totally interested. I just know I shouldn't be. Not yet.

Her nose scrunches. "Why on earth not?"

"Because."

"Just because?"

"Yes, just because." I know it's lame, but it's all I've got. Honestly, I have never been caught so off guard by a man before, and I'm pretty sure I just waved the proverbial white flag in front of him.

"Let this play out, babe," Gaston says, capturing his wife's attention. She looks up at him and opens her mouth like she's going to argue, but he covers her lips with his thumb, cutting her off. "Let it play out."

"Fine," she mumbles against his finger; then her eyes come to me, and his finger drops away.

"Go have lunch with your husband," I tell her before she can ask me the hundred questions I see in her eyes. "I'm good here and will be even better if you happen to stop somewhere on your way back and pick me up a burger with fries."

"Anna—"

"Babe, let's go get lunch," Gaston cuts in, and she bites the inside of her cheek as she looks at me, the door, then back again.

"Don't make Gaston carry you out of here. I'm good. Just go have lunch and feed that baby." I look at her belly as she rests her hand on her stomach in a protective gesture. I know from our talks that she's nervous about becoming a mom, but I have no doubt she's going to be one of the best moms around.

"Okay," she agrees reluctantly. "And I'll bring you back a burger, but later, you and I are going to talk."

"I can't wait," I joke, and Gaston laughs, wrapping his arm around her shoulders and leading her outside. When they're gone, I close my eyes, wondering how I can feel equally scared and excited about the idea of seeing Calvin again.

Suggestion 3

Don't Get Your Hopes Up

Anna

I place a carton of strawberries in my cart, then look at the shopping app on my cell phone, checking them off before scanning the rest of the list. Growing up, I never went to the grocery store. I just put what I needed on the housekeeper's list, and like magic, it would appear the next day. In college, I didn't cook or shop very often. Then later, when I got my own place, I used a service, so everything was delivered. And I did that after I moved in with Lance, because it was easier with both our busy schedules. I wouldn't have thought I'd find wandering the aisles and picking things for myself enjoyable, but there is something relaxing, maybe even fulfilling, about the simple task of making a list and going to the grocery store.

"Anna." I lift my head and frown when I see a woman I don't know walking toward me, quickly pushing a cart that seems to be overflowing with food. She's smiling like we know each other. "You're Anna, aren't you?"

"Yes . . . have we met before?" I ask, trying to place her. Since I started working at the bakery, when I'm out and about around town

I often run into people who've come to the shop, but she doesn't look familiar.

"Oh Lord," she says with a laugh as she reaches out to grasp my arm. "Please excuse my manners. I'm Elsie, Calvin's mom."

Calvin's mom. Holy cow. My heart drops into my stomach.

"Pearl mentioned you had red hair and that you were very pretty, so when I saw you, I just knew it was you." She shrugs, giving my arm a squeeze before dropping her hand away. "So what are you doing here?"

"Umm . . ." I automatically glance at her shopping cart and mine, and she laughs, catching me off guard with the exuberant sound.

"You're shopping. Of course you're shopping. What else would you be doing at the grocery store?" She waves her hand like she's wiping away the question.

I giggle, unable to control it, and her eyes brighten with humor. "Sorry," I say.

"For what? Laughter is the best medicine." She presses her lips together briefly. "At least that's what the plaque in my kitchen says."

"Are you sure you're Calvin's mom?" My eyes widen, and I want to snatch the question back, but it's too late. It's already out. "Sorry, I mean . . . he's awesome, great really. It's just—"

"Don't apologize," she says, cutting off my rambling. "I know my son can be a little gruff. He's like his father in that way, but I promise once you get to know him, you'll find out he's also sweet."

Sweet? I wouldn't describe Calvin as sweet. I'd describe him as hot, forward, and aggressive. Or maybe he's just hot, and the rest was just the impression he gave me the last time I saw him, a week ago. Not that I'm counting the days or disappointed he hasn't kept his promise of seeing me again.

"Trust me: he's a big softy."

"I don't really know your son that well, but I'm sure you're right," I say while fighting the urge to laugh. Even not really knowing the man,

I can imagine what his reaction would be to his mom describing him as a softy.

"It's so funny running into you here," she chirps, and something in her eyes causes me to instantly go on guard. "I was going to call Pearl and ask her for your phone number. She mentioned you don't have any family in town, and I'm having a barbecue tomorrow. I wanted to invite you over, since there will be lots of people there."

"I . . . oh . . . well, I . . . that's very nice," I stutter out, then add a touch of defeat to my tone. "I would love to come, but tomorrow I have to work."

Her expression falls but then turns hopeful as she asks, "What time do you get off work?"

"Around five."

"That's perfect." She claps, making my pulse jump. "You can come over after you get off, since we won't even start the grill until a little before then."

"I . . ." I start to say I can't, but with the way she's looking at me, I can't force the words out. What the heck is happening right now, and why do I feel like I'm being played? Not wanting to hurt her feelings, I say the only thing I can. "I would love to come."

"Great." She digs into her bag, which is sitting in the front of the cart, and continues talking. "I'll just take your number and text you my address." She pulls out her phone, then waits for me to rattle off my number. A moment after she types it into her cell, my phone rings. "That's me. Just ignore it for now and store it when you have a chance." She grins, then leans toward me. "This must be serendipity: me wanting to invite you over, then running into you today."

"It must be," I agree.

Her smile seems to grow, and she touches my arm again. "It was nice meeting you, Anna, and I'm looking forward to tomorrow."

I'm not sure I agree, especially if her son is going to be there. "Is there anything you want me to bring?"

"Nope, I've got it covered." She waves her hand over the cart she's still holding on to with one hand. "Just bring yourself and your appetite." Her phone rings in her hand, and she looks at the screen, then me. "Sorry, I need to take this, but I'll see you tomorrow."

"See you tomorrow." I get one more smile from her before she walks away, putting her phone to her ear. I shake my head; then, with nothing else to do, I finish shopping and head home, not sure how I feel about what's just happened.

Following the directions on my phone, I turn left and then start to look for somewhere to park when the automated voice tells me I've reached my destination. The entire street is packed with cars, which makes me wonder if everyone parked on the street is going to the same barbecue I am. I finally find an empty space down the block, shut down the engine, and pull down the visor to look at myself in the mirror. I knew I would be coming here right after work, so I brought a change of clothes to the bakery and am now wearing a pair of cute black linen shorts, a white tank, and my favorite wedge espadrilles.

Frowning at my tired-looking reflection, I grab my purse from the passenger seat and dig through it for my travel makeup bag. I carefully add a couple of swipes of mascara to my lashes, a little blush to my cheeks, and my favorite berry-tinted lip gloss. Once I'm done, I pull in a breath and let it out slowly, then get out of my car and grab a box of cookies and bars from my trunk.

As I walk down the block, taking in the moderate-size homes and the trees lining the streets, I wonder if Calvin grew up here. Or if he rode his bike down this street. Or parked on the block when he was in high school, away from his parents' house, so he could have a few more minutes to make out with whatever girl he was dating at the time—something that I imagine changed frequently. I scan the house numbers until I reach a white house with dark-blue shutters, flowers lining the walkway, and a huge hot-pink summer-themed wreath on the door with a large flamingo drinking from a martini glass in the center. I walk toward the front door, picturing Elsie outside wearing a big floppy hat and gloves, playing in the dirt each spring and fall, tending to the yard. It's a task my mother wouldn't be caught dead doing. Not when she could pay someone to do it for her.

"Let me help you with that," a man says, and I turn to find a good-looking guy who appears about my age with blond hair and brown eyes coming up the steps behind me.

"It's okay. I've got it." I smile, and he shakes his head while taking the box from me before opening the door to the house like he's been here before.

"Are you coming?" He stops to look over his shoulder, and I step into the house and close the door while looking around. The living room and kitchen are open, and the space looks welcoming, with paintings and quotes on the walls and knickknacks along with framed photos on every available surface. "Everyone is out back. Come on."

I start to follow him, then stop when Elsie appears from around the corner, spotting him first. "Todd." She leans up, kissing his cheek. "I thought you said you'd be here two hours ago."

"Sorry, Mom. I got caught up at work."

"You're always getting caught up at work." She frowns at the box he's holding.

"She brought them." He tips his head my way, and I wave when her head turns in my direction.

"Anna." Her frown slips away as she smiles. "You're here, and I see you met my youngest, Todd."

"I did." I smile, and he returns it before he goes to a butcher-block island just inside the kitchen and sets down the box.

"Is Dad out back?" he asks.

"He's at the grill," Elsie tells him, and he shakes his head, then lifts his chin toward me.

"Nice meeting you, Anna."

"Nice meeting you too." I watch him walk away, trying to find even a small similarity between him and his brother, but there doesn't seem to be one—at least not in the looks department.

"Are you hungry?" Elsie asks.

"I'm always hungry."

"Then you're in the right place." She heads into the kitchen, and I follow, stopping when she peeks into the box I brought with me. "Did you bake these?"

"My boss made the cookies, but I made the bars."

"They look delicious." She takes out one of the caramel-cream bars and smells it before taking a bite. "This is very good. I'll have to get the recipe." She closes the lid on the box, then nods toward a door. "You can put your purse in there while I grab some stuff from the fridge."

"Sure." I place my hand on the door handle and push before jumping back when a huge brown dog rushes toward me.

"Bane!" she shouts as the dog knocks me to my bottom and proceeds to lick my face, making me laugh.

"Bane, stop! Oh God, Anna, I'm so sorry," Elsie says, finally pulling Bane off me. "Calvin has some big case he's been working on this past week and hasn't been home, so Bane has been staying with us. He must have gotten locked in the room the last time someone went in there."

"It's okay." I get up from the floor and laugh when he comes back over to nuzzle his face into my stomach. "Is he a German shepherd?"

"Yeah, Calvin's been training him so he'll be able to go out on patrol with him. But unlike what he told you about his dog listening, he obviously lied."

My cheeks warm. "He told you about that?"

"Pearl told me, and I told him to find you and apologize for what he said."

"Oh." Well, that answers why he came by the shop, and now I feel like an idiot for thinking he felt the same pull I did when we met and couldn't stay away.

"Enough about that. Let's put your bag up, get you a drink and some food, and introduce you to some people." She takes my purse from my hand and places it on the bed, then walks back by me. "Do you mind helping me carry some stuff outside?"

"Not at all." I give Bane's head another rub, then follow her to the fridge with him at my side. Once our arms are full with condiments, she opens the sliding door, allowing the sound from outside to pour in.

"Everyone here is either family or a close friend. You don't need to be nervous."

"My parents used to have get-togethers at least once a week. I'm used to being around people I don't know. I'm out of practice, but I'll be okay," I reassure her.

"Where are your parents?" she asks, eyeing me with curiosity.

"Chicago. They both were born and raised in the city."

"Have they come to visit you here?" she asks.

"Not yet," I say, not wanting to tell her the truth—that my parents have pretty much disowned me since I called off the wedding and moved. At first, they seemed convinced I'd gotten cold feet and would come back in time. When I didn't return after three months, they threatened me with the loss of my inheritance. Now they're just giving me the cold shoulder. They don't call or check in, and when I reach out to them, they get off the phone as quickly as possible or ignore my calls completely. It hurts, but I can't say I'm surprised by their actions, since neither of them would ever win an award for parenthood.

"Tell them to come at the end of the summer when there aren't so many tourists," she says as we step out onto a large deck that overlooks a swimming pool where kids are playing and people are lounging. As large as the backyard is, it looks miniscule with so many people packed into the space. "Honey, this is Anna. Anna, my husband, Drake," Elsie says. She takes the things from my hands and places them on the table next to the grill. I focus on the very handsome black man with a beer in one hand and a skewer in the other she's motioning to.

"Nice to meet you, Anna." Drake drops his beer to the table so he can stick out his hand toward me.

"Nice to meet you too." I look between him and Elsie, then at Todd, who's standing next to his dad.

"She's got the look, babe," Drake says, holding my gaze, and Elsie laughs.

"Drake and I couldn't have kids, so we adopted Calvin when he was five and Todd when he was two."

"I—" I start to apologize for possibly offending them but am cut off when Todd gasps.

"I'm adopted? Why didn't you ever tell me?" he asks, looking between his parents, cutting the tension I'm feeling immediately.

"Oh, stop." Elsie rolls her eyes at him, then looks at me. "We're used to people being curious, and so are the boys. Since the day we brought them home, we've been open about their adoption."

"Plus, it's not like they'd be able to keep it a secret for long," Todd adds, patting his dad's shoulder.

"I don't know. You two have the same eyes," I say, and Todd looks at his dad with admiration.

"I guess you're right," he agrees, and his father wraps his large hand around the back of his son's neck in an affectionate gesture. "Do you want a drink, Anna?" Todd asks when his dad lets him go.

"I'll have a wine cooler, if you have one."

"I already like her." Drake grins, lifting his own wine cooler toward me, and my chest warms.

"Honey, set her up with a burger. I'm going to take her down by the pool and introduce her to everyone," Elsie tells Drake, and he turns toward the grill, placing a patty of meat on the bottom rack.

"I see you've been claimed," Todd says, handing me a wine cooler.

"Pardon?" I ask, confused. He tips his head down, and I follow his eyes to Bane, who is sitting at my feet. "I guess you're right." I rub the top of Bane's head, and he leans into my side, resting his weight against me.

"Don't even think about it, bud. Your brother already called this one," Drake says, which I find odd.

"I know." Todd rolls his eyes at his dad.

I want to ask what they're talking about but am distracted when Elsie threads her arm through mine. "While that's cooking, let's go mingle."

"Sure." I smile at both men, then let her lead me down the steps to the lower yard and pool. I stand at her side as she introduces me to every single person who's there. By the time we make it back up to the grill, my burger is cold and my wine cooler is empty, but my soul feels full, because everyone is genuinely nice and welcoming.

With the sun starting to set and the outside lights glowing, I grab another drink and walk through the grass to find an empty table under one of the huge trees in the backyard and set down my drink and plate before I take a seat. I smile at a couple as they walk by, not catching even a hint of fakeness when they smile back. Unlike whenever I attended my parents' parties, I don't feel out of place or like I'm pretending to be someone I'm not. Surrounded by these people, I get to be myself—Anna, a woman who is new to town and works at a bakery—and it feels good to be accepted for me, not because someone is attempting to befriend me so they can get in my parents' good graces.

I take a sip of my drink, then pick up the fresh hamburger that Drake insisted on making me and take a huge unladylike bite. I then look over my shoulder when I hear the grass crunching behind me.

"Are you having a good time?" Todd asks as he takes a seat next to me, and I pick up my napkin and cover my mouth as I chew and swallow.

"Sorry, yes, it's been fun. There's a lot of people here." I grab my wine cooler and take another sip, conscious of the fact that I have to drive home tonight.

"I know Mom is a little overwhelming, but you'll get used to it." I raise a brow, not sure what he means by saying I'll get used to it. "Mom has a sense. She's always adopting new people, which is why there are so many people here." I look around, stopping on Elsie, who is standing next to her husband and smiling at whatever he's saying as he talks to a group of people sitting a few feet away. "They legally adopted Calvin and me, but they foster kids whenever one needs a place to stay, and Mom is always bringing new people into the fold."

I swallow, not sure why my throat suddenly feels so tight. "Your mom is amazing."

"Yeah," he agrees softly, looking across the yard toward his parents. "They both are. Plus, you won't find a better man than Calvin." He gets up, taking his beer with him. "It was nice meeting you, Anna. I'm sure I'll see you around."

I start to open my mouth to call him back so I can tell him that his brother and I aren't even friends and that I'm not sure I'll be at another one of his parents' barbecues, but the hairs on my nape stand on end, and Bane, who hasn't left my side, gets up and starts to wag his tail. Knowing even without looking who's just arrived, I attempt to get my nerves to settle and my stomach to stop dancing, but it's impossible.

"Good boy," I hear rumbled, and I look over my shoulder just in time to watch Calvin squat down to greet his dog with an affectionate rubdown. "I missed you too." He scratches the top of Bane's head, then lifts his eyes, locking them with mine.

Staring into their blue abyss, I feel transfixed. It's odd to have such a strong pull to someone I don't know, but I feel drawn to Calvin in a way I have never felt with a man before, and that totally freaks me out.

"Anna."

"Calvin." He stands, and Bane circles his feet as he walks toward me.

"You look beautiful." His hand comes to rest on my shoulder, but it's not his touch that catches me off guard or even his words; it's the way he's looking at me. The way his eyes have warmed and filled with a look that makes me feel desired, a look that makes me feel like I'd be safe with him. "I was surprised when my mom told me you were here."

"Were you really?" I ask as he takes a seat across from me. Having experienced the whirlwind of meeting his mom and spending the evening with her, I get the feeling she tends to run over people to get what she wants—although not in a bad way.

He looks toward his parents and smiles, slightly shaking his head. "Maybe not. I should have known she'd go after you herself after she told me where you worked," he says, picking up my wine cooler and taking a large gulp.

"Please, help yourself," I say sarcastically, eyeing my drink in his hand.

"Don't mind if I do." He lifts it to his lips once more.

I roll my eyes at him, then pick up my burger and take another bite. As I chew, I look down at my lap, then place my hand on Bane's head as he rests it on my thighs, looking up at my hamburger and me.

"Don't give me that look," I tell him, and he lifts his head, placing his snout closer to my hand.

"Bane, don't beg," Calvin orders, and Bane eyes him, then looks at me.

"Sorry, pup, but you can't have any," I whisper, and he lets out a loud huff, then falls to the ground, sprawling his legs out before him and dropping his head to his paws.

"Did you have a good day at work?" He leans forward, placing his elbows on his knees. A move that doesn't just bring him closer but also envelops the air around me with his warm, masculine scent.

I look away from him, feeling my cheeks heat up, and clear my throat. "It was good."

"Do you work tomorrow?"

"Why?"

His lips tip up slightly. "Just making conversation."

"Then no, I don't work tomorrow," I reply, and he opens his mouth like he's about to say something more, but just then his phone rings.

He leans back and pulls his cell from the front pocket of his jeans. His expression fills with frustration when he looks at the screen. "Sorry, I need to take this."

I nod and he gets up, moving a few feet away and placing his phone to his ear. I try to hear what he's saying but can't make out his words over the music playing from the sound system that surrounds the pool. I pull my attention off him to look down at Bane, who's watching him, and take a bite of my burger as I try to force myself to relax.

A moment later, I feel a hand rest on my shoulder and tip my head back. Calvin's eyes drop to my mouth; then his index finger curves around my chin, and his thumb sweeps the edge of my lips. "Ketchup." He pulls his hand away and places his thumb in his mouth, making my insides squeeze. "I gotta go."

I swallow hard and try to ignore the disappointment I'm feeling. "Is everything okay?"

His expression warms. "Yeah, just work."

I nod again, unsure what to say.

"I'll see you soon. Get home safe." He turns and walks off, patting his thigh for Bane to follow. I watch the two of them go, confused by the mixed emotions swirling inside me.

Suggestion 4

NOTHING IS BY CHANCE

ANNA

"Are you a mermaid?" I open an eye and lift my hand to block the sun, which is so bright it's almost blinding. "Are you?" I'm asked by an adorable, chubby little girl who's squatting down next to me. She looks to be about four, with blonde hair in two pigtails, and she's wearing a hot-pink polka-dot swimsuit with frills around her waist.

"No." I smile at her as I sit up.

"Your hair looks like mermaid hair."

"I know, but sadly, I'm not a mermaid," I say, then wonder if I should have lied when her expression falls. "Where are your mom and dad, honey?" I look around. The beach isn't empty, but there still aren't many people out, and no one has come close to where I've been lounging all afternoon.

"Over there." She points down the beach toward a couple who look to be asleep under an umbrella. "They're taking a nap."

Irritated that they've left her unsupervised, especially so close to the ocean, I push myself up off the ground and hold out my hand toward her. "Come on. I'll walk you back over to them."

Her eyes drop to my hand, and she shakes her head. "I'm not supposed to go with strangers."

Great, well, at least she knows that. Maybe her parents should have told her not to wander off.

"My name's Anna. What's yours?"

"Amy." She drops her eyes and kicks her foot through the sand.

"Okay, Amy, let's go wake up your parents. I'm sure they'll be worried if they wake up and you're not around."

She tips her head back and crosses her arms over her tiny chest. "I want to go swimming."

"Okay, let's go wake up your parents so they can take you swimming," I prompt, and she shakes her head and takes a step back.

"I want to go swimming." She stomps her foot.

"Amy." I try to add a tinge of warning in my tone, but it comes out more as a plea.

"No, I want to go swim!" she yells, then turns and takes off toward the water.

"Amy, get back here!" I run after her as she heads right toward the surf, and then, with no other choice, I follow her into the water. I start to panic when a large wave sweeps in, knocking her backward before dragging her out with it. I pick up speed, scanning the water around me, and then spot the top of her head coming up before she disappears once more. With my heart lodged in my throat, I dive under the surf and kick as hard as I can in her direction, praying I'll be able to find her.

It's difficult to make out much of anything, even though the water is clear and the sun is shining. I need a breath before I pass out, so I shoot up to the surface and gasp for air while looking around. My lungs seize when I feel something brush against my leg. Hoping against hope, I dive once more and scan the darker water below for any sign of what I just felt touch me.

I spot Amy's hair waving through the water, and relief and fear make me dizzy as I grasp her limp hand and pull her toward me. I kick as hard as I can toward the surface, and the moment I break the top, I gasp for air and look at her pale face. "God, please," I whimper. I shout for help and shout for her to wake up as I swim toward shore. The moment I feel sand under my feet, I start to walk through the water with her in my arms, not even realizing people have started to gather along the water's edge.

"I've got her," an older man says, trying to take her from me, but my hold on her tightens.

"She's not breathing." I shake my head, then repeat, "She's not breathing."

"I know. I'll help her." He places his arms under her limp body, and I let him take her from me, then watch as he runs the rest of the way out of the water before dropping to his knees in the sand and placing her on the ground. My knees wobble as I watch him start to give her CPR.

"Come on, dear." I look over at an older woman wearing large shades and a big hat as she places her arm around my waist in an attempt to hold me up when I start to fall.

"EMTs are on the way," I hear someone say, and I look around the crowd, then down the beach, where I spot Amy's parents still asleep under the umbrella, even with all the activity going on.

"Her parents." I shiver, even though I'm not cold.

"Pardon?" the woman asks, adjusting the big floppy hat on her head.

I stumble away from her with my entire body shaking. "She needs her parents. They're sleeping."

"I don't understand." She follows me, even as I start to run.

When I reach where the two of them are lying, I rip their umbrella out of the ground, and they both instantly sit up. "What the fuck, bitch?" the guy snaps, and anger like I have never felt in my life surges through me.

"Your daughter is over there!" I scream while swinging my arm out to the crowd, which is growing by the minute. "She's getting CPR, because you two idiots weren't looking after her."

The woman's face pales; then she and the man both jump to their feet and start to run. I stumble behind them through the sand, hearing sirens getting closer, and then my legs give out from under me when I hear someone shout, "She's breathing!"

"You saved her," the woman who helped me earlier says while resting her hand on my back, and I look at her as my vision blurs. "Are you okay?"

Am I? I don't know.

"You don't look so good."

"I'm okay." I try to stand, but my body feels weak and my vision seems to be growing dimmer by the second. "I live right there." I point toward my apartment, which is only a little ways up the beach.

"Let me help you up." She weaves her arm through mine, and I use her strength to pull myself up off the ground.

"Thanks. I think I've got it from here." I blink, trying to get rid of the stars and darkness that are sweeping over me.

"Darling, I know you think you're okay, but I think you should sit down and rest for a moment," she says, eyeing me with concern.

I wave her off. "I just need to get my stuff and go home. After I rest, I'll be fine." I take two steps and hear a gasp right before everything goes black.

"Everyone back up!" A deep, familiar rumble drags me through the darkness toward consciousness.

"Is she okay?" a somewhat familiar woman's voice asks.

"You said she just passed out, right?" Warm fingers touch my neck; then a large hand comes to rest on my chest.

"Yeah, she looked pale but said she was okay, but then her eyes went weird and she kind of toppled over."

"She rescued that girl," a male voice says, and I try to open my eyes as everything comes back to me. "She's probably in shock."

"She said she lives right there," the woman adds as I force my eyes open but then close them against the bright light. "She was going to go home."

"Is Amy okay?" I ask, wondering why my throat hurts and feels like I've eaten sand.

"Get me some water."

Calvin? My muscles bunch, and I open my eyes to find Calvin leaning over me.

His gaze locks with mine; then his fingers slide down my cheek.

"Hey, beautiful."

"Oh God." I close my eyes, hearing him chuckle.

"Can you sit up for me and rinse your mouth out?"

I nod, not wanting to talk, and then I let him help me sit up. When he puts a bottle of water to my lips, I take a sip and swish it around before leaning over to spit it out, trying to do it as inconspicuously as possible.

"You fell face-first into the sand." I look to the woman at my side as she pushes my hair out of my face. "I didn't have time to catch you."

"It's okay," I tell her, then start to cough when my throat itches from the sand I've apparently ingested.

"Drink and spit again," Calvin orders, holding the bottle closer to me once more, and my cheeks warm as I do as he commands. "How are you feeling?"

I focus on his handsome face and don't even lie when I answer. "Like I swallowed sand and ran a marathon."

"I bet." He touches my temple, then slides his finger down the side of my face to behind my ear.

"You didn't answer. Is Amy okay?"

"She was breathing when they put her in the ambulance. They think she'll be okay," he says, but I still see a glimmer of worry in his eyes, and that makes my chest ache.

"You saved her," the woman says, taking my hand and attention. "If it wasn't for you following her in, no one would have known what'd happened to her."

My eyes burn and I swallow over the lump in my throat, not sure how to respond.

"Let's get you home," Calvin murmurs, and then, before I have a chance to prepare myself for what's about to happen, he places one arm behind my back and one under my legs and lifts me up off the ground. I instinctively wrap my arms around his neck and squeeze. "I won't let you fall, babe, but you need to let me breathe." He sounds like he's laughing.

"I can walk."

"I'm not taking any chances. Plus, I need to talk to you about what went down today."

"What do you mean?" I ask, squirming to look at him.

"From what I understand, after you got the girl out of the water, you had a confrontation with her parents."

Damn, I forgot about that, with everything else that happened and the whole passing-out thing. "It wasn't really a confrontation."

"Then you can explain exactly what it was after I get you home."

"Great," I mumble.

"Wait, her stuff! You're forgetting her stuff!" the woman yells, rushing toward us while holding on to her hat, with my bag over her shoulder and my towel floating behind her like a flag. Calvin stops for her to catch up, and once she's standing before us, she hands me my things. "I'm Maxine. Everyone calls me Max. I come here all the time, so I'm sure I'll see you around."

"Fuck me," Calvin grumbles, and I wonder what that's about but don't have a chance to ask him before he snaps at her, "This story is not going in the paper, Max."

Wait . . . what? "Of course it's going in the paper." She waves him off. "People like a feel-good story."

A feel-good story? What does that mean?

"I would love to chat with you, but I gotta go check on my husband," she says before spinning on her heel and quickly walking away.

"Maxine!" Calvin bellows, but she acts like she doesn't hear him, and I know it's an act, because everyone within a mile radius probably heard him shout her name. "Fucking shit."

"Umm, what just happened?" I ask as he starts to storm toward my place.

"She's going to write about what took place today," he tells me on a low growl while tightening his hold.

"Is she an author?"

"No, she's a reporter for the local paper, the *Seaside Post*."

"Oh." I turn to look behind us and spot Max walking toward the man who took Amy from me to give her CPR, and I wonder if he's her husband.

"This is a tourist town, babe, but the people here are all locals, which means everyone and their mother is going to know what went down. And all those people are going to want to thank you in person."

My nose scrunches up, partly because I don't believe him, but really because I don't relish the idea of having to deal with that kind of thing. "She doesn't know my name."

"Yet."

"What?"

"She doesn't know your name yet, but she will know it by the end of the day."

"How?" I lean back to frown at him.

"First, there aren't many women in town with your hair. Second, there aren't *any* women in town as beautiful as you with your hair."

Butterflies take flight in my stomach at the compliment. "I'm not sure those are really ways to find out my name."

"Yeah, then think about the fact that she knows where you live." He shakes his head, then tips his head to the side. "Can we take the stairs up, or do I need to carry you around front?"

I notice then that we have already reached the warped and worn wooden stairs that lead up to my apartment.

"They're safe, but I can make it up them alone." I attempt to wiggle free, but he shakes his head, adjusting the hold he has on me.

"You can think that all you want. I'm still not putting you down."

"Are you always so stubborn?"

"Yes."

"Why am I not surprised by that answer?" I sigh in frustration, then squeeze my eyes closed when he starts up the stairs. When he makes it to the top, I let out the breath I was holding and then ignore the disappointment I feel when he sets me on my feet.

"Do you have your key?"

I don't answer. I dig into my bag, and when I finally grasp the cold metal, I attempt to unlock the door, but my hands are still shaking, making the task seem impossible.

"Let me help." His warm hand covers mine, and he gently takes the keys and opens the door, then waits for me to enter before he follows me in. I drop my towel and bag to the floor near the door, not wanting to drag sand through the room, and then I walk to the kitchen, pick up a glass, and flip on the faucet. I lean into the counter for support, willing my hand to stop shaking, and then flip off the lever and down the glass in just a few gulps.

"It's shock."

"What?" I look at Calvin as he places his hip to the counter a couple of feet away and crosses his arms over his wide chest.

"You passed out from shock. Your body dumped loads of adrenaline into your system to give you the strength you needed to get the girl out of the water, and when that was done, it crashed. It's normal after a high-stress situation."

"How long does it take for the shakes to pass?"

"Depends. It can take a couple hours or a day. You'll likely dream about what happened, too, and that might cause another adrenaline spike and the shakes to return. The good thing is eventually they will go away."

"That's good," I agree, filling the glass once more.

"What you did was brave."

"I did what anyone else would have," I say, and he tips his head to the side, seeming to study me more closely.

"Did you know the little girl?" he asks, and my brows drag together, and I shake my head. "Then you're wrong. Someone could have wanted to save her, but they might not have gone through the lengths you did to do it."

"I didn't do anything," I say, leaning into the counter, not sure if my legs will be able to hold me up much longer.

"The people on the beach said they saw you go into the water and watched you go under, not coming up for what seemed like minutes before going under again and again, then finally appearing with her. Max was right: you saved her."

"But did I? You said she was breathing. You never said she was awake."

"You're very observant," he says, studying me in a way that makes me feel like he's trying to figure me out.

"I had to learn at an early age how to read between the lines. A lot of times, people tell you what you want to hear. Still, they always leave hints so that if they're ever caught and things are brought to their attention, they can say they never lied."

"Have you been lied to a lot?"

"No, but I've been told a lot of half truths." I shrug, taking another drink.

"I see." He nods, and for some reason I think he does.

"So what did you need to talk to me about? Do I need to fill out a report or something?"

"No report, but I do have a few questions about how you came to know Amy, and your interaction with her parents."

"Can I sit down?" I ask. My legs feel like jelly, and there is no way I want to seem weak around him. Falling on my face again would for sure make me seem weak.

"Yeah."

I walk past him to my bed and take a seat on the edge, wrapping my arms around my bare middle. I frown as he walks toward my front door, and I start to ask what he's doing but stop myself when he grabs one of my hoodies off the hook and brings it to me. I glance down at myself, wondering how I could possibly forget that I'm not dressed, that all I have on is my bikini.

"Thanks." I take the gray sweatshirt from him when he holds it out to me, then quickly pull it over my head and tug it down to cover the tops of my thighs.

"Now, why don't you start from the beginning?" he prompts, leaning back against the wall in front of me, making me feel small.

"Can you sit down?" I blurt, then quickly add, "It's just . . . it feels like an interrogation with you hovering like that, and—"

"You don't need to explain." He slides to the floor, and then, with his legs bent and his wrists resting on top of his knees, he asks, "Better?"

I lick my lips, not sure I like this position any more than the previous one. Honestly, I don't know if him being anywhere in my place would feel okay. The room is too small for his large presence, and with my bed taking up most of the space, it makes this feel too intimate, especially with the conflicting emotions he brings out in me. Who am I kidding? I'm not conflicted; I'm just crazy, because he's the first guy

I've ever wanted just because I want *him*—not because he checks a box or fulfills certain criteria.

"Anna."

I jump slightly and focus on him. "Sorry." I lick my lips. "From the beginning?"

"Yeah, baby, from the beginning. And take your time."

I drag in a breath, then tell him everything that happened. I start from the moment Amy asked if I was a mermaid and end at the moment I passed out. More than once, I pause, because his anger seems to engulf the room, making it almost hard to breathe. But he always reassures me that he's okay before urging me to continue. When I'm done, he stands, and I grab hold of his hand before he can disappear, like he has a tendency to do. "Can you find out about Amy for me?" I feel desperate for good news. I want to know she's okay.

"As soon as I know something, I'll let you know." He slides his thumb over my pulse, and I swear it skips at the touch.

"Thank you." I try to let his hand go, but his fingers tighten around mine.

"I'm going to give you my number. If you need to talk, call me; I don't care what time it is."

"I'll be okay," I assure him.

He shakes his head. "Anna, I have no doubt you will forever be okay. What I want you to know is that I'm here if you need to talk, no matter the time."

"Okay," I agree, and he releases my hand. He reaches into his back pocket and pulls out his wallet to take out a card.

My fingers grasp it, but when he doesn't let go, I look up at him, and his voice is so soft, so regretful, when he speaks that I feel the sincerity in each word. "I wish I didn't have to go, but I need to get to the station to file some paperwork."

"I understand, and seriously, I'll be all right," I say, and then my lips part in surprise when he leans down to touch his to my forehead.

"I'll see you soon, Anna."

I don't nod or say a word. I watch him walk to the sliding door, open it, and close it behind him, and then I continue to watch him through the glass until he disappears out of sight as he heads down the steps to the beach.

I fall back against my bed and rub my eyes, trying to remember if I ever had so much excitement in my life before I moved here. I don't think I did. Really, my life in Chicago was pretty boring, considering everything that's happened recently.

"Anna Belle!"

I jump up when my name is shouted and run to my front door when Edie starts to pound on it. I swing the door open, and my knees weaken when I see the look on her face.

"What happened?" I ask, startled by her expression.

"You're okay!" She wraps her arms around me, squeezing me so tight I can't even breathe.

"Edie, you're freaking me out."

"I'm freaking you out?" She leans back and shakes me from side to side. "I just heard what happened and rushed home to make sure you're okay."

"I'm fine," I tell her softly, pulling her in for another hug. "I'm just a little shaken up."

"Honey." Her voice cracks. "Those tides can be tricky. You could have died out there."

My throat gets tight, and tears burn the backs of my eyelids, because I still don't know for sure that Amy is okay.

Edie leans back to look at me, then slides a piece of hair behind my ear while tears form in her eyes. "You, my beautiful girl, have a warrior's soul, and today you proved you're not just willing to take risks to benefit yourself. You're willing to take risks to help others, and that is true bravery." She smiles slightly, and tears fill my eyes. Her thinking I'm brave means everything. It means more than she could ever know.

"No tears." She leans in to kiss my cheek, then grasps my hands. "Now, go shower and meet me downstairs for a glass of wine."

I look at the clock on the oven. "It's not even two."

"If you take one lesson from today, let it be that you should live every single day of your life like it's your last. Drink when you want, laugh until your soul is full, open yourself up to falling in love, spend time with people who are important, and enjoy every moment, even the scary ones."

"Like you, Pearl, and Dixie," I say softly. That's exactly how they live their lives.

"Like us but better, because you're still young enough to do it right from the start." She smiles, then pushes me gently away. "Now, go shower while I find us the perfect bottle of wine."

With my throat tight, I start toward my bathroom but stop when I hear the door open. "Edie." I turn to face her.

"Yeah?"

"I love you," I tell her quietly. "Thank you for everything: for believing in me and for just being here for me. I don't know what would have happened if you weren't placed in my path."

"You would've been okay, child, but I hope you know I love you too."

I nod, then watch her go, knowing that even with everything that's happened, I have no regrets, not a single one. Every day I'm getting closer to finding myself and the happiness I've been searching for.

With that last thought in my mind, I take a shower, then go meet my friend for a glass of wine that we drink outside under the warm sun. The sound of the ocean is the background to our relieved tears after Calvin calls to tell me that Amy woke up and will be okay.

Suggestion 5

FAKE IT UNTIL YOU MAKE IT

ANNA

"Maybe I should reconsider giving you days off, because it seems a lot happens when you're not here at the shop," Chrissie says, picking up a bouquet of flowers off the front counter and handing it to Gaston. He's been loading them into his car off and on all day to take to the local retirement home.

"Or you could just thank me for making this the best day of the year in terms of sales." I smile cheekily as Gaston laughs while I walk into the back room to take a pan of cupcakes out of the oven and grab a tray of cookies. The display case is almost empty. Calvin was right about Max finding out my name. What I didn't know she would do was put my name, along with where I work, in the article, claiming I was some kind of hero for rescuing Amy.

"What are you planning on doing next?" Chrissie asks as I come back in, carrying the tray.

"I don't plan; I'm more of a 'live in the moment' kind of girl," I tell her as I bend down to place a fresh tray of cookies in the display case.

"Is that so?"

As I hear Calvin ask that question, my head flies up, and I'm sure I look like a deer caught in headlights. I didn't hear the door chime when I was in the back, and Chrissie didn't even give me a heads-up that he was here.

"I'm going to help Gus take out some of these flowers. We'll be back in a few minutes," Chrissie says, and then the door chimes, announcing she and Gaston have left, but I don't pull my eyes off Calvin's. I can't.

"Why are you looking at me like that?" he asks, walking toward the counter. He's dressed almost exactly like he was the first time we met, in dark jeans and a button-down shirt that's form fitting and accentuates his powerful build. His appearance, along with the look in his eyes, causes my heart to pick up speed as he gets closer.

"How am I looking at you?"

"Like you can't decide if you want to run to me or away from me."

I shift on the balls of my feet, wishing I were better at keeping my emotions locked away. "Why are you here?" I ask instead of answering his question.

"I wanted to come check on you. I tried to call you last night, but you didn't answer, so I called Edie. She said you fell asleep in her guest room. And you haven't answered my calls today or responded to my text."

Edie told me when I woke up this morning that he'd called her, and every time I saw his number on my phone today, I tried to talk myself into answering or calling him back. I just couldn't force myself to do it, even though I really wanted to.

"Thank you for checking up on me. As you can see, I really am okay, so you don't need to worry about me," I say, watching as his eyes flash with frustration and his jaw tics.

"Christ, you're good."

"What?" I say with a frown, confused by that statement.

He comes a step closer and leans into the counter with both hands. "I've never met a woman quicker than you are at putting up walls. You're good, Anna. So good I bet no one ever gets in."

"Don't be a jerk."

"You shouldn't be surprised I'm calling you out on whatever game it is you're playing, since one minute you're sweet and vulnerable, and the next you're sour and on guard."

"I'm not playing a game." I cross my arms over my chest.

"No? Then what are you doing? Why are you pushing me away?"

"I'm not pushing you away." I shake my head like his statement is completely ridiculous . . . but it's not. He's right; I have been pushing him away, because it's easier than acknowledging I like him, especially when I don't know if I'm ready to like anyone.

"Then what are you doing, Anna?"

"I'm not doing anything, Calvin."

"Lie."

"I'm not lying."

"Then explain to me why you're so set on pushing me away."

"I don't know." I toss my hands in the air, getting frustrated.

"You don't know," he repeats.

"When it comes to you, Calvin, I don't have a clue what I'm doing."

"And that scares you." It's a statement, not a question, and my back straightens.

"Don't be absurd. I'm not scared," I lie.

"Then what do you call it?" he asks, capturing my hand and startling me with his firm grip. "If you're not scared of me, then what is it?" He coaxes me closer, causing my breath to turn choppy.

"Nothing," I whisper, dropping my gaze to his lips, which are close—so close I know all I'd have to do to feel them against mine is lean in an inch.

"Do you want to kiss me, Anna?"

My stomach dips, and the word *yes* rests on the tip of my tongue as he runs his nose across mine, making my stomach dip and my toes curl.

"I want to kiss you," he whispers.

Oh God, I want that too. I have never wanted to kiss someone more than I want to kiss him.

"Calvin . . ."

"I want to see you tonight."

"Okay." My eyes widen; I'm surprised that I've just agreed so easily when I've been so careful about sticking to my decision to not date. His pupils dilate as my heart starts to pound. "I mean—"

"Don't take it back," he rumbles, and then his lips brush mine softly, causing my eyes to slide closed as my breath catches in the back of my throat. I feel him pull away, and my lashes flutter open to find him watching me. "I don't know what has you so scared of me, Anna, but if you have the ability to rescue a little girl from the ocean, you can face your fears regarding me. We'll talk tonight. Over dinner, you can tell me about your life before you moved here, and maybe then we can figure out together what's holding you back. And if you're open to hearing it, I'll share a little about my past. You're not the only one who's nervous about doing this, but I feel in my gut that it will be worth it."

My stomach rolls with nausea at the idea of him knowing the kind of person I used to be, and the lengths I was willing to go to make my parents happy. If I ever told him about my past, he wouldn't want anything to do with me. Maybe that's the real reason I've been attempting to keep him at arm's length. "Maybe we—"

"We'll talk tonight." He cuts me off before I can make up an excuse to postpone seeing him. "I'll be at your place at six." He steps back from the counter.

"I'm not sleeping with you," I tell him firmly, even as my cheeks warm with embarrassment. "I can meet you somewhere."

He grins. "Anna, get your mind out of the gutter. I'm bringing dinner. We'll eat and talk, and hopefully you'll be able to keep your hands to yourself so we'll have a chance to get to know each other." I press my lips together to keep from laughing, but still my lips twitch, and a look of pleasure fills his gaze. "I'll see you tonight, okay?"

I drag in a breath, knowing I should say no. But when I open my mouth, "Okay" comes out again.

"Later, beautiful." He turns to the door as it's pushed open by Chrissie, with Gus right behind her. I study her goofy smile and wonder if she was standing out front with her nose pressed to the glass, watching our exchange. Knowing her, she was. There's no way even her husband would be able to stop her from spying on Calvin and me.

"Are you leaving already?" she asks Calvin.

Gaston shakes his head. "Chrissie, baby, let the man go. You watched them kiss. They obviously don't need your help."

"I didn't watch them kiss." She gasps in outrage, spinning around to face her husband.

"Babe."

"Don't *babe* me." She shoves his shoulder, then turns to Calvin, who's watching the exchange and trying not to laugh. "I didn't watch you kiss her."

"She kissed me," Calvin states, and I look at him and narrow my eyes.

"I didn't kiss you. You kissed me."

"Did I?" He shrugs. "I don't remember."

"Oh my God, you're so . . ."

"Amazing?" he finishes for me.

"No. You're a—"

"Awesome."

"Annoying," Chrissie inserts, and I smile at her, even though she's not looking at me.

"You should plan on hearing that a lot," Gaston tells Calvin. Then he adds, "But word to the wise—never tell them they're being annoying. Trust me. That will not go over well for you."

"Maybe you should stop while you're ahead, honey, because at this point, you're working toward sleeping on the couch with LeFou." Chrissie glares over her shoulder at her husband.

"See what I mean?" Gaston grins as he wraps his arm around her shoulders, then kisses the side of her head.

"Maybe there *is* something in the water, making men more annoying than usual," Chrissie says.

"It's probably the moon. Edie was saying something about the moon being almost full the other night," I say, and Calvin laughs.

Chrissie snaps her fingers. "That's it. It has to be."

"Well, I think that's my cue to go," Gaston says, turning Chrissie to face him. "I'll see you at home." He grasps her face between both his hands to kiss her, then leans back, rubbing his thumb against her cheek. "After I drop off the flowers, I'll pick up dinner. Just send me a text to let me know what you want."

"Thank you."

"Anything." He touches his lips to her forehead, then turns to smile at me. "Later, Anna."

"Bye, Gaston, and thanks for taking the flowers."

"Flowers?" Calvin asks.

"Anna's been getting flowers all day and didn't want them to go to waste, so she asked if Gus could take them to the local senior home."

"Max ran the story. Did she use your name?" Calvin sounds pissed, and my brows draw tightly together.

"Yeah, you said she would," I remind him.

"Yeah, and I went to her and told her that if she used your name, she and I would have problems."

"Obviously she didn't listen to you. We haven't seen the article, but at least a hundred people came in today asking for Anna directly, saying they'd read about what she did in the paper," Chrissie says, and I bite my bottom lip when anger infuses Calvin's features.

"Fuck," he growls, jerking his fingers through his hair, and then he turns to me. "I'll see you tonight." When I nod, he looks at Chrissie and Gaston. "Later." He swings open the door.

"Wait!" I call, and he turns to look at me over his shoulder. "Where are you going?"

"I'll see you tonight." He walks out, seeming to be on a mission as he storms past the windows and down the sidewalk.

"What's that about?" Gaston asks.

"My guess is he's not happy about his woman's name being in the paper," Chrissie replies with a dreamy sigh.

"I get that," Gaston agrees.

"I'm not his woman," I inform them, and Chrissie slowly turns toward me and grins. "Don't grin at me like that."

"Like what?" she asks, still smiling.

"You know what."

"He's protective. I think that means even if you're not his, you still are," Gaston says, and I glare at him. "Just sayin'."

"Aren't you supposed to be leaving?" I ask.

"Are you going to let her kick me out?" he asks his wife, trying to sound offended.

"Absolutely." She pats his chest. "While Anna and I finish closing down the shop, we're going to talk about what's going on with Calvin and her, and she won't open up if you're here."

"There's nothing to talk about. He's just coming to my place for dinner. That's it."

"That's how it starts," she informs me, and I groan. "Trust me. First it's just dinner, and the next thing you know, you're living together and having a baby. And if you don't trust me, you can always ask Leah how things progressed between her and Tyler."

"Now I really am gonna go," Gaston murmurs, gaining her attention by kissing the top of her head. "I'll see you at home."

"See you at home." She leans up, touching her mouth to his, and then she watches him walk out the door like he's going off to war, not running a few errands. I have to admit: they have something most people don't have. The admiration and love they have for each other is rare, especially nowadays. Even Lance, who claimed to be in love with me, would go days without calling if he was away on business. And even when we worked in the same office building, he never came by to bring me lunch or see if I wanted to grab some with him.

"Now that he's gone, let's talk about Calvin," Chrissie chirps, flipping the **Open** sign to **Closed** and locking the door.

"I didn't lie," I tell her, opening the register to pull out the tray of cash so I can do a count. "We're just having dinner." I frown. "I'm still not sure how I agreed to have dinner with him."

"Did he ask you when he was talking to you over the counter with his face close to yours? Because if it was then, I would have been distracted too."

"You really were spying on us." My lips twitch into a smile.

"I wanted to make sure you were okay." She shrugs, then eyes me with curiosity. "It looked like you enjoyed the kiss."

"It wasn't really a kiss—more of a brush of lips," I say, trying to downplay it, because I haven't even had the chance to come to terms with the way I reacted to such a small touch of his mouth to mine. I haven't kissed a lot of men, but even with the ones I have, I've never felt it to my toes.

"You really are working hard to make things between the two of you seem insignificant. Why is that?" she asks softly, and I stop what I'm doing to look at her.

"The truth?" I ask, and she nods. "I don't know if I'm ready to put myself out there with someone, and honestly, I don't think he will like me very much if he finds out about my past."

"Your past?"

The only person who knows the truth about my parents, the reason I was getting married, and then why I decided to move here is Edie. Chrissie knows I was engaged, but she doesn't know the full story. I chew the inside of my cheek, then let out a deep breath, hoping I'm doing the right thing by telling her. I would hate it if she wanted me to quit or looked at me differently.

"My parents are pretty wealthy, and they wanted me to marry someone of the same status. I got with my ex because he had money, not because he was a good guy or because I liked him."

"Anna," she whispers, and I'm surprised there isn't even a small hint of disgust in her tone.

"I don't like that I did that. I'm not proud of the person I was," I say as my stomach churns with nausea.

Her expression softens. "Can I ask you something?"

"Of course," I say quietly, hating that this is a conversation we are having.

"Was he a good guy, and did you like him?"

I don't even have to think about it. "He was very nice, and I did like him. I just wasn't in love with him; I never was. I was just comfortable with him. What we had was easy. We both just kind of lived our lives. There wasn't any real passion between us."

"And you think he didn't know that?" she asks, and I must look confused, because she continues. "Sweetie, if you think a man can be with a woman and not recognize when things are not like they should be, you're wrong. You might have agreed to marry him for your own reasons, but it seems to me that he had reasons of his own for wanting to marry you too."

Did he? "He loved me." I frown.

"Did he tell you that?" she asks, looking disbelieving.

"Yes."

"Did you tell him that you loved him?"

My stomach drops. "Yes," I whisper.

"Do you understand the point I'm trying to make?" she questions softly.

"I think so."

"People date for all sorts of reasons. Some people only want to date the most attractive members of the opposite sex, even when they have nothing in common, because it makes them feel better about who they are. Some men only want to date younger women, because they want to feel superior, and some women only want to date men who are financially stable, because they don't want to worry about money. You and Lance got together because each of you met a need for the other. There is nothing wrong with that. Who knows? You both could have spent the rest of your lives content with what you had. The only thing is . . . you wanted more. You wanted to be in love and assumed he wanted that too."

She looks away, shaking her head. "I know you." Her gaze comes back to me. "I know he said he loved you, but I have to say, if he did, he would've been here trying to convince you to come home. That's what Gus would do if I told him I was leaving, and I know Tyler would do the same with Leah. When you love someone, you don't just let them give up on the relationship."

I stare at her, stunned. I've never thought of it like that. I always just assumed he was in love with me, because he said he was. Now, I'm not so sure. When I told him I was calling off the wedding and ending our engagement, he didn't plead with me to stay or even ask me why I didn't want to be with him anymore. Looking back, he didn't even seem surprised. At the time, I just assumed he was trying to make things easier for me, but now I'm wondering if he didn't fight because I really didn't matter to him, because our relationship didn't really matter to him.

"I think you're right," I whisper, unsure how to feel. I don't have the right to feel used by him, but if I'm honest with myself, I do. "I don't think he loved me. I mean, I think he cared about me, but I don't think he was in love with me."

"Only he knows that. The only point I'm trying to make is that I can see you're interested in Calvin, and there's no doubt in my mind that he's interested in you. So maybe it wouldn't be a bad thing to give him a shot to see where things go."

"He scares me," I admit, fiddling with the pockets of my apron.

"I bet he does."

"Like, *really* scares me," I say. Even thinking about him makes me feel anxious.

"That's because you're attracted to him. You'll get used to it." She grins.

"Will I?"

"Look at Gaston. I never would have thought a man like him would ever want me, but with time, I came to accept he did, and it didn't hurt that he was so sure of things between us from the beginning. I think, given the opportunity, Calvin will be the same way. All you have to do is give him the chance to prove himself to you."

"Why on earth would you think Gaston wouldn't want you?" I ask, flabbergasted by that comment.

"Why are you scared of Calvin?" she returns.

"Point made."

She shrugs. "We all have our issues to work through. Lucky for me, I found a good man who was willing to hold my hand while I worked through my own personal doubts and insecurities. I know I would be okay without him, but having him makes everything better. He gets me, even when I don't get myself."

"I'm glad you found that with him."

"You'll find it with someone too. It might be Calvin, or it might not. The thing is, you will never know unless you try, so at least see what happens with him. Give him a real chance and trust him to take care of you."

"I'll see what happens," I agree, even though the thought of opening myself up to someone really scares the crap out of me, and I get the feeling that Calvin won't accept anything less than the truth, even the ugly parts. I just hope that when I do open up, he won't think less of me.

Suggestion 6

TRUST YOUR INSTINCTS

CALVIN

When I reach the parking garage for the *Seaside Post*, I try to talk myself down from losing my shit on Maxine before I get out to head inside. Maxine is right; Anna is a hero, but the story isn't as cut and dry as she made it seem.

Yesterday, after I left Anna's place, I went to the station and filed a report regarding the negligence of Amy's parents. Even understanding the stress they're under, having almost lost their daughter, they still need to be held accountable for the role they played in what happened to her. If the two of them hadn't been asleep, chances are she wouldn't have been able to wander off. Then Anna wouldn't have had to risk her own life to save a little girl she didn't even know.

After I filed the report, I called Maxine and urged her to leave the names of those involved out of her story, especially considering the open case and CPS looking into Amy's parents, who happen to be well known in the area. Her father is part of the city council and is the mayor's son, and her mother is a trophy wife who runs a few local charities when she's not getting her nails and hair done. Maxine was already at her desk when we spoke, and she told me that it was her right to print what she wants. It's a fact I couldn't argue, but after I told her she would never get another story from me or any of my men again, she assured me that she would leave names out.

She lied to me. Not only did she use names, but she talked about both of Amy's parents napping while their daughter almost drowned and Anna's reaction to finding them still asleep after she got Amy out of the water.

I pull open the door to the building and scan the open space. The newspaper offices used to be a textiles warehouse years ago, but the textile company went out of business and the local paper moved in. Seeing Maxine at a desk in the back corner, I head in her direction with the paper still in my grasp.

I shouldn't be as pissed as I am. Years as a police officer have taught me the media isn't always your friend, and you need to be prepared for whatever case you're working on to be leaked. My anger isn't about the story. My anger is about her sharing Anna's name after I specifically asked her not to. Why that's so important to me, I don't know.

"Max." I stop at the side of her desk and slam down the paper, making her jump. "I thought you and I had a deal yesterday regarding using Anna's name," I growl, leaning closer to her.

"Calvin." She leans back in her seat, smiling, looking unsurprised, like she's been expecting me. "I wasn't going to run her name, but when I realized who she was, I had to."

"Who she is?" I stand back, crossing my arms over my chest and waiting for her to continue.

"Her family is legendary in Chicago. Her father is a McAlister and a multibillionaire. She was engaged to Lance Erwin, heir to a multimillion-dollar company." Fuck. My insides twist as her reasons for being so standoffish become clear. "With that information alone, I had to run the story. Then I found out she called off her engagement a few months ago and canceled their wedding plans—an event that was supposed to rival the display we saw when Harry and Meghan got hitched in London. After she did that, she ran off to our little town, moved into a room above Edie, and got a job at a bakery. From what I've learned, no one knows exactly why she left, but her parents have disowned her, and all of her friends—or those she once had—are torn between hoping she finds what she's looking for and wondering if she's crazy for giving up the life she had."

"You didn't have to run her name, Max. You wanted to for attention."

She shrugs. "You're not wrong. She's news—*big* news."

I see a calculating glint in her eyes, and my muscles bunch. "Max, please tell me you're not going to write another story about her."

"Why not?" She tips her head to the side. "She's basically royalty."

"She's not royalty. She's a person who left her life behind for a reason, and if she's not telling you that story herself, it's hearsay."

"I talked to enough people today who were close to her to know it's not hearsay." I glare at her, and she holds my gaze for a moment, then looks away. "I have work to do, so if that's all, I need to get back to it."

"You run that story, me and my boys will never take another one of your calls, Max, and I mean that."

"The good news, Calvin—I'm retiring this year. I won't ever need to call you again."

My jaw clenches, and my hands ball into fists. Fuck. I want to throw something, but instead of doing that and possibly losing my badge, I turn and storm across the room and out the building.

Once I'm in my truck, I turn on the engine and wonder what the fuck it is I'm going to do. Anna left her life behind for a reason. What that reason is, I have not a fucking clue. All I know is I need to warn her about what's about to go down, then figure out how I'm going to deal with the fallout. She might not care that Max knows her story, but I have a feeling she's going to care that I do. From the moment I first approached her, she's been skittish and has used every excuse to avoid me, and this might give her a reason to cut me out completely.

I back out of my parking spot and head toward town. I have an hour before I'm supposed to be at her place. It's enough time to go get Bane and pick up dinner, but not enough to go to the station and use my computer to find out whatever information I can about her life before she came here. I thought shit was complicated before. Now I know I was wrong. That said, I'm not willing to just walk away. The pull I feel to her is too strong, and I learned early on in life to follow my gut. My gut is telling me that I need to explore things with her.

When I reach my house, I go inside and sigh when Bane greets me at the door. One of the couch cushions is in the middle of the entryway, and white fuzz hangs from his jaw.

"Seriously?" I ask, and he lies down, dropping his head to his paws in an attempt to look innocent. "I thought we were past this stage." I start to scoop up the fuzz that's littering the floor, then pick up the cushion to see if it's salvageable. It's not; the hole is huge. I carry it through the house to the kitchen and shove it into the garbage. After I get everything cleaned up, I look at my dog, who doesn't look like a puppy anymore but obviously still is. "Come on—you're coming with me."

I pat my thigh and head back out the front door with him excitedly bouncing at my side. I let him into the cab, then go around and get in behind the wheel. I call in an order for a half-plain, half-everything pizza on the way, then stop and grab a case of beer from the gas station before I go pick up the pizza. I reach Anna's place twenty minutes later at five after six and notice Edie sitting outside on her porch swing when I get out. Taking the pizza and beer with me, I call Bane to follow.

"I thought for sure I'd be seeing this exact thing a week ago. You work slow, Calvin," Edie teases as I walk up the driveway.

"Had a case come up, or I would have been here a week ago," I inform her.

"Good to know you're late because of work and not because you're an idiot who's stuck in the past." She smiles, then stands. "Gonna take my old bones inside. Have a good evening, and be good to my girl."

She walks to her door and goes inside without another word, and I shake my head.

When I reach Anna's landing, I knock and look down at Bane, who's sniffing and whining to get in. "Down," I order, and he falls to his bottom as the door opens.

"Hey." Anna eyes me nervously, then laughs when Bane jumps up, placing his paws on her chest.

"Bane, heel," I growl, and he licks the side of her face before landing on all fours.

"I see training is going well," she says cheekily, smiling at Bane as he wanders into her place with his nose to the ground.

"You're lucky my hands are full, Anna. If they weren't, I'd kiss that smart mouth," I say, and her eyes flare while her cheeks turn pink. I step inside when she steps back, and I notice again what I saw yesterday. Her place is small: just big enough for her bed and a little table in the kitchen area that's pressed to the wall, with two chairs on either side. There's a lone painting of the ocean on the wall, and a couple of gray-blue throw pillows on the bed. Everything else is white. I know Edie used to rent the space out during peak seasons, which made her enough money to keep her fed and warm through winter. I imagine it doesn't look any different now than it did then. There are no personal touches in the room, nothing that shows that a woman as vibrant as Anna lives here.

"Do you want to eat out on the deck?" she asks, taking the pizza box from me and setting it on the counter.

"Yeah." I hold up a beer. "Want one?"

Her nose scrunches adorably, and she shakes her head. "I'm not a big fan of beer, but I have wine. I just need to open the bottle."

She pulls a bottle of pink wine from the fridge, and I take it from her. "Where's your opener?"

"I can open it."

"I know." I still take the corkscrew from her and open the bottle, then pour her a glass.

"Will Bane be okay out on the deck, or should we leave him inside?"

"He should be okay. Then again, I got home today to find he'd eaten half a cushion from my couch, so I don't know what to expect from him right now."

"He ate a cushion?" She looks to where he's nosing the ground. "Is he okay?"

"It's not the first time. This is just the first time in a while. He should be fine."

"How old is he?" she asks, lifting up on her bare feet to grab plates off one of the open shelves.

"He turns two next week." I lean back against the counter with my beer and take a moment to appreciate the way her hair looks down, the dip of her waist, and the way her ass looks in her jeans.

"Then he should be out of the puppy stage soon." She grins at me over her shoulder. "My mom got one of those little yippy dogs when I was about sixteen, and he was annoying and destructive until he was about two and a half."

"Good news for me."

"Yeah." She tips her head to the side. "Do you want to carry the pizza out?"

"Lead the way." I pick up the pizza and follow her out to the deck, where there's a small table and two adirondack chairs. I place the box on the table and take a seat while she does the same before handing me a plate. Once we both have a slice of pizza and Bane is settled near the top of the steps, I break the comfortable silence that's settled between us, even though I don't want to. "I went to talk to Max today."

"I had a feeling that's what you were doing when you left the shop this afternoon," she says quietly, and I focus on her, hating what I'm about to say. "You warned me she was going to run the story."

"I knew she'd run the story, but I thought she and I had an agreement that your name would be left out."

"I'm not in witness protection, Calvin. It's not a big deal she used my name. I mean, it was weird having people come into the shop asking for me and acting like I'm some kind of savior. But I think we both know that tomorrow I'll be old news, and people will be moving on with their lives. I'm just happy Amy is okay."

She's wrong, so fucking wrong. "She knows who you are, Anna."

My jaw twitches with frustration when she smiles, clearly not understanding what I mean. "I know."

"No, baby. She knows who you are. She knows who your family is." Her eyes close, but I continue. "She knows about your fiancé and that you canceled your wedding." Her face loses color, and the anger I felt earlier comes back full force. "She's planning on publishing your story, and there is not one fucking thing I can do about it."

"I . . . I . . . I don't even . . ." She shakes her head. "Why? Why would she do that?" she asks, and I take her plate before she drops it, because her hands are shaking, and set both our plates down. "She can't do that . . . can she?"

"I'm sorry, Anna."

She sits forward, pushing her fingers through her hair and making her red curls look even wilder. "Why would she want to write about that?"

"Your family is loaded. Your ex is, too, and you ran away from them to live here and work at a bakery."

"I left because I wanted to be happy," she says, like she's talking to herself. "I wanted to be near the ocean. The few happy childhood memories I have involved the beach. It was as if the ocean had the power to bring out the best in my parents." She turns to look at me, and I fight the urge to pull her into my lap to hold her, to comfort her. "Thinking about it now, it might have been the only time they were ever happy, the only time I was ever allowed to be me. That's why I left Chicago;

I realized I was going to end up just like them. I was going to marry a guy I wasn't in love with and spend the rest of my life living a lie." She looks away, and when she speaks again, the pain she's feeling is audible. "Maybe you should go. Maybe you coming here was a bad idea."

"I'm not leaving." The words are rough, and she turns to eye me warily when I take her hand. "Knowing you have a past hasn't changed the fact that I want to get to know you."

"Was your past ever splashed all over the town's local paper without your approval?"

"No, but I grew up here, so I'm sure at some point you'll hear a story or two about me."

"What kind of stories?" she asks, dropping her gaze to my thumb as it rubs across her wrist.

"I was a rebel growing up. I was always pushing boundaries and getting in trouble."

"That's surprising. I would have guessed you always followed the rules."

"I wanted my parents to prove they loved me enough to stick around, regardless of how shitty I was," I tell her truthfully. "I don't remember my birth parents—not much about them, really—but them abandoning me became a part of who I was, who I am, and when I was a kid it made me feel insecure."

"Calvin." She turns her hand in mine and grasps my fingers.

"You'll probably hear about me and my ex at some point too. I was with her for several years. I thought we were working toward spending the rest of our lives together, but she realized that she couldn't live a life where her future husband missed events and was out all night because of work."

"I'm sorry."

I shake my head. "I don't want you to feel sorry for me," I tell her, looking into her eyes. "I just want you to know that we both have pasts. The things we went through led us to who we became and where we are. I'm not saying it's going to be easy dealing with the fallout from whatever story Max makes up, but at the end of the day, it doesn't matter what anyone else thinks. You did what you felt you had to do," I say, watching her eyes fill with tears. "No tears. For now let's forget about the article until it's time to deal with it and just enjoy our cold pizza and this view."

"Okay," she agrees, and I lift her hand and kiss her fingers. I let her go and give her plate back before settling in my chair with mine. "I know we're supposed to be done talking about it, but do you know what's annoying?" she asks as I lift my pizza to take a bite.

"No."

"It's annoying that I haven't spoken to my parents in weeks, since they haven't been taking my calls, but I have no doubt that if they catch wind of this, they'll call me faster than a duck can swim upstream." She lifts her wineglass and downs a gulp. "That's annoying."

"I think you mean downstream."

"What?" She frowns at me as she sets her glass down.

"Faster than a duck can swim downstream."

"Does it really matter what direction the duck is swimming?"

My lips twitch. "No, I guess not."

"Exactly." She waves her hand around before taking a bite of pizza.

"Why haven't you talked to your parents?" I ask before lifting my beer to my lips.

"You haven't heard?" she questions sarcastically. "I ran away from Chicago and ended my engagement to the perfect guy."

An emotion I'm not comfortable with settles in the pit of my stomach. I shouldn't be jealous, not when she's not mine and obviously still trying to come to terms with what happened. Still, there's no denying that the feeling in my stomach is jealousy. "The perfect guy?"

At my question, she looks at me, and her eyes widen like she's just realized what she said, and she shakes her head. "He was the perfect guy for them, not me."

"How's that?" I ask, not understanding.

"Because I didn't love him. Because he didn't make me happy."

"Why was he the perfect guy for them?" I prompt, and she looks away for a moment.

When her eyes come back to me and she speaks again, her voice is soft and filled with regret. "I don't think we should be talking about this."

"Why not?" I should let her off the hook, but I want to know what led her to being engaged to a man she admits she didn't love.

"Because I kind of like you, and I don't want you to think less of me."

"I won't think less of you," I tell her sincerely.

"You can't say that, Calvin. You don't know the lengths I was willing to go to earn my parents' love and make them happy."

"You were going to marry him to make your parents happy? Why would marrying him make them happy?"

"Because he had money."

"And why did you get into a relationship with him?" I ask, and she looks away. "Anna."

"The truth is I thought the first time I met him that he was different. He didn't talk about money all the time. He didn't seem to care about who my family was. He was nice and easygoing, and I thought I could love him."

"Why would that make me think less of you?"

Her eyes come back to me, and I can see she's uncomfortable. "I stayed with him even when I knew I didn't love him. I stayed because he had money, and that was what was really important."

"Why did you need to marry someone wealthy? Max said your dad is a billionaire."

"He's not." She snorts. "Between his spending and my mom's, his part of the inheritance, which was split among him and his siblings, has dwindled down to a little over five million. And considering their lifestyle, that's a drop in the bucket. No one knows about my parents' money issues. Everyone just assumes they're loaded, because that's the image they project."

"If they have five million dollars, I wouldn't say they have money issues, babe."

"That's because you're normal. You probably wouldn't even consider spending hundreds of dollars on a single dinner out, thousands of dollars on a weekend vacation, or more money than most make in a year on a new car or handbag."

Hearing that and knowing that's a life I will never live—and don't even desire to live—I ask, "Are you normal?"

"I don't know who I am," she answers quietly, moving her eyes to the ocean. "I like going out to dinner, but what's the point of having a nice meal if you don't enjoy the company you're keeping? I like vacationing, but I don't need a five-star resort. And I like nice things, but they don't make me happy." She picks her glass back up and takes a sip of wine, then settles back in her chair. "All I want is to be happy—really happy."

"That's what everyone wants, Anna, so I think that makes you normal."

"Are you happy?" she asks, pulling her eyes off the view in front of us to look at me.

I dig deep for the truth, not wanting to lie when she's been so honest. "Mostly."

"Mostly?"

"I love my job and my life, but like everyone, I want more. I want to find someone to build a family with, and more time with my parents and brother. I'm not sure I'd be completely fulfilled having all those things, but I think they'd add to my happiness."

"Simple," she whispers, studying me intently.

"Pardon?"

"What you want is simple." She smiles sadly. "It's not money or some new gadget or car; you want simple things, things that are easily achievable, things that are actually important at the end of the day."

"And what do you want?" I ask, not even realizing that I'm holding my breath as I wait for her answer.

"I don't know." She shrugs one shoulder. "I don't know what will make me happy. All I know is it's not what I had before I came here."

"Are you any closer to finding it now that you're here?"

She lets out a long breath. "I love living here. I enjoy my job. I wake up every day and can look at myself in the mirror without hating myself. I'm starting to feel settled. So I guess the truthful answer is, I think so."

"Good, baby," I say quietly. I'm not sure I've ever met a woman like her before, a woman who is capable of admitting things that might be uncomfortable to talk about, things that might make people look down on her. Her honesty is refreshing.

One side of her mouth tips up. "You know the worst of me, Calvin, so if I don't hear from you after tonight, I don't even have to question why that is."

"You won't get rid of me that easily, Anna." I hold her gaze, amazed by her strength. Most people would lie or paint things differently, and not many women would open up about their past the way she just did. "You feel up to going for a walk down on the beach with me?"

"I'd like that," she replies, and I stand, then take her hand and help her up.

Once she's in front of me, I touch my lips to her forehead before leaning back to catch her eye. "Thank you for opening up to me." Her eyes fill with surprise, and she gives me a nod. "Come on."

I lead her down the wooden steps to the beach, then stop to take off my shoes and fold up the legs of my jeans, ignoring my cell when it rings. Once I'm standing, I take her hand and walk with her into the surf, sighing when my phone rings again.

"Do you need to take that?" she asks, kicking her foot through the water as Bane jumps along a wave rushing on shore.

"It's just work." Normally, I don't mind getting calls when I'm off duty, but right now I'm tempted to toss the phone currently ringing in my pocket out into the ocean.

"Your mom mentioned the other day that you have some big case. Could it be about that?"

"Probably." I watch as she tucks her hair behind her ear.

She stops and turns so we're facing each other, and I look down at her beautiful freckled face with the wind blowing in her hair that's shades of red and orange in the dusky light. "Calvin, you can take the call, and if you have to go, we can do this another time." Fuck, I have never wanted to kiss a woman more than I want to kiss her. "Seriously, it's not a big deal." She smiles.

"Anna, shut up." I drop my mouth to hers, cutting off her gasp of outrage, and tangle my fingers into the hair at the back of her head. She instantly falls into the kiss, moving her hands up my shoulders to hold on and opening her mouth.

The first flick of my tongue against her tongue drives the kiss deeper, wilder. I hold her closer, wrapping my arm around her back to keep her against me, and then trail my lips to her ear and down her jaw, and I nip her collarbone. Her whimper drives me close to the edge, but I fight against falling and drag my mouth away from her delicate skin. I tuck her face into my neck, willing my body back under control as we both try to catch our breath.

"Did you tell me to shut up?"

I dip my chin down to grin at her. "Babe, you talk a lot."

"So you did tell me to shut up," she mumbles. I chuckle, then curse under my breath when my phone starts to ring again. "Take the call." She places her hands against my chest. "It could be important."

I don't want to, but she's right. After letting her go with one hand to reach into my pocket for my phone, I glance at the screen and see Herb's name, and then I swipe and put it to my ear. "This better be good," I say to my partner.

"Sorry, Cal, I know you're off duty—someone came in and said they have information about your murder case."

"Who?"

"Sandy Burton."

"Sandy." I shake my head, figuring this is another dead end. I went to high school with Sandy. We didn't hang with the same crowd, but she was always sweet, which hasn't changed over the years. She works as a local beauty pageant coach and, as during our high school years, still tends to stick to herself. My murder victim was a young man with no ties to the area, and I doubt Sandy would have been near an area heavily populated with clubs, which is where the victim partied the night before his body was found. "All right, put her in the room and let her know I'll be there within the hour."

"I'll tell her, and see you then." He hangs up, and when I shove my cell back into my pocket, I notice Anna's body has gone rigid against mine.

I look down and see that some of the pink has left her cheeks, and her eyes have gone blank. "I gotta go."

"I heard. Was that . . ." She jerks her head from side to side. "I mean . . . are you investigating a murder?" she asks, and I'm honestly surprised she hasn't heard about the murder in the media.

"I can't talk about my work." I rub my thumb across her smooth cheek, curious if she's soft everywhere.

"Of course. I don't know why I asked. I've watched enough television shows to know that you—"

I kiss her, cutting off her rambling, and then drag my mouth from hers. "I think I like that way of shutting you up." Her eyes narrow, but before she can speak, I do. "Do you work tomorrow?"

"Maybe."

I sigh, taking her hand. "I thought we were past that."

"Then we're even, 'cause I thought we were past you being a jerk," she tells me, sounding put out, but something about her tone lets me know she's joking.

"Kissing you makes me a jerk?" I say with a smile.

She looks at me out of the corner of her eye. "No, the 'shutting up' thing does."

I stop and turn her toward me, then dip her back over my arm to touch my lips to hers.

When her eyes flutter open, I smile. "I don't know. It seems to me that you don't mind it much."

"You're annoying." There's no heat in her words.

"And you're stunning." I stand to my full height, bringing her with me, and then turn to search the beach for Bane. I call for him to come when I spot him wandering off down the beach with his nose pressed to the ground. He lifts his head to search for me, then runs at full speed, kicking up sand and making Anna laugh as he skids past us and stumbles over his four legs.

When we get back to her stairs, I bend down to put my shoes back on, then look up at her when she asks, "Do you want to rinse your feet off in the shower? I know it's no fun walking around with sand in your shoes."

"Yeah, thanks." I carry my stuff up the steps and grab what's left of the pizza, along with my empty beer, while she picks up her wineglass. I follow her inside and place the pizza on the table.

"The bathroom's down the hall. Towels are on the shelf above the toilet."

I go to the bathroom, surprised by the amount of color packed into the small room. The bright floral shower curtain is the first thing to catch my attention, and it matches the towels, folded neatly in an alternating rainbow of blue, orange, purple, and yellow. I don't even bother shutting the door. After rinsing the sand away, I put on my socks and shoes, then go out and find Anna in the kitchen, standing with her back to me and watching Bane drink water from a large bowl she set down.

"I know you can't talk about work, but will you let me know once you get home tonight?" she prompts, not even looking at me as I walk toward her.

"Yeah," I reply quietly.

"Thanks." Her head turns, and her eyes meet mine over her shoulder. "And thanks for the pizza."

"You never told me if you're working tomorrow." I get close to her side, and our fingers brush.

Her eyes search mine before she answers softly, "I'm off."

"Do you like fishing?"

"Fishing?" Her brow furrows. "Do you mean fishing with a pole and worms?"

I can't stop my smile. "Yeah, fishing with poles and worms."

"I've never been," she says with a slight shrug of her shoulder.

"You'll like it. If you don't have plans tomorrow, you can come with me."

"Okay."

"I'll pick you up at five."

"When you say five, do you mean five at night or five in the morning?" she asks, looking skeptical.

I turn her toward me and rest my hand on the curve of her hip. "Morning."

"I'm not sure that's a good idea. I'm not really a morning person."

"I'll bring coffee." She stares at me, unblinking. "Lots of coffee," I amend.

"What about doughnuts?" she asks.

"Coffee and doughnuts."

"I guess I'm going fishing," she says with a sigh, making me laugh.

I kiss her lips, trying to remember if I've ever been this affectionate with another woman. I don't think I have. With no time to figure out what's so different about her, I look at Bane. "Time to go." He swings his head between Anna and me, then walks to her, nudging his nose into her palm. Once she's rubbed his head, he wanders to the door, ready for a new place to explore. "I'll see you in the morning."

"See you in the morning." She gives me a shy smile as I open the door, and I leave, fighting the urge to kiss her again.

Suggestion 7

ENJOY THE MOMENT

ANNA

Wearing jean shorts that are folded at the hem, plain white sneakers, a T-shirt, and a hoodie, I sit at the end of my bed and stare at the wall while wondering what the hell is happening in my life. Since the moment I moved to town, I've been working on acknowledging the mistakes I've made in my past and on trying to be a better person. I've been honest with those who are close to me about why I moved here and have been able to stand tall and answer their questions. But I don't know if I will be able to do that if the *Seaside Post* runs another story about me. I don't know if I will be able to handle people looking at me differently—especially those who have come to mean so much to me.

A knock at the door interrupts my thoughts, and I open it, frowning at Calvin's smiling face.

"Morning." He looks far too handsome and awake, especially when the sun hasn't even risen.

"Coffee." I cover my mouth to hide a yawn, and his smile turns into a full grin. I didn't lie when I said I wasn't a morning person. I hate mornings. Actually, mornings aren't bad if they are spent in bed or lazing around the house. But it always seems to take a whole lot of coffee to get going in the mornings if I have something to do or somewhere to be.

"It's in the truck." He takes my bag. "Do you have your keys?"

I pull them from my hoodie pocket, and he takes them from me and locks the door before leading me down the stairs to a double-cab black truck with dark-tinted windows. Once we're both in and buckled, he hands me a large metal tumbler that's warm to the touch.

"That should be enough coffee to hold you over until we stop for breakfast."

I take a sip of coffee and sigh as the warm, sweet, creamy liquid hits my tongue and slides down my throat. He laughs softly as he reverses out of the driveway, and once he puts the shifter in drive, he takes his hand off the stick and rests it on my thigh.

I take in the veins, the scar near his thumb, and his blunt nails. His hand looks masculine in comparison to my smooth skin, and I like the way it feels. Really, I like how it feels anytime he touches or kisses me. It doesn't feel fake or forced; it's not out of habit or duty. Each time, it's felt natural, like it's always been that way, which is odd, considering how our relationship started and the length of time we've known each other.

"How far are we driving?" I ask, trying to get my mind off the way the warmth of his palm is radiating up my leg, making parts of me tingle.

"She speaks." He glances over at me, his eyes twinkling with humor. "That only took twenty minutes. I thought for sure it'd be at least an hour." He squeezes my thigh affectionately, and I jump, almost dropping my coffee, as a bolt of desire hits me square in my core. "You okay?"

I lick my lips. "Yeah . . . yep." I shake my head. "Just still trying to wake up. I'm not used to being up so early."

"I'm used to early mornings. I forget that not everyone else is," he says. "We got about an hour drive ahead of us. You can sleep if you want. There's a blanket in the back seat."

I look into the back seat, grab the blanket, and then ask, "Where's Bane?" I don't know why I didn't notice he wasn't with us before. Maybe because I wasn't really awake.

"With my partner. He took him home last night. He wants to do some training with him today. I'm sure that was a lie—his kids have known Bane since he was a pup, so they like when he's around, and Herb likes to give them what they want."

"That's sweet of him," I say, then chew the inside of my cheek. I want to ask him what happened last night after he left my place, but since he said he couldn't talk about work, I don't think that would go over well.

"I can hear the wheels turning in your head. I can't talk about work, especially when the case is open, but the woman who came forward last night didn't know anything I didn't already know."

"I'm sorry."

"It happens. It sucks when it does, because you never know what will lead to a break in a case or who might know something. Unfortunately, I'm still at square one."

"I don't think I could be a cop." My heart wouldn't be able to deal with seeing the worst parts of human nature up close or the lack of humanity some people display.

"It's not always easy," he agrees as I settle the blanket over my lap and his hand, still on my thigh.

"How long have you been a police officer?" I ask him, leaning the seat back slightly.

"Since I was twenty-two. When I graduated high school, I enlisted in the military and served four years. When I got out, I moved home and joined the force, then went back to school and worked my way up to detective."

"How old are you?" He doesn't look older than thirty, but I learned early on that looks can be deceiving. My mom is in her sixties and looks forty, tops. I mean, that's with surgical help and Botox, but still.

"Thirty-three, or I will be in two weeks. What about you?" He glances at me quickly.

"I'm thirty. My birthday was a month ago."

"You look closer to twenty-five."

My nose scrunches. I've always hated looking younger than I am. When I was twenty-one, I looked eighteen, and no matter where I went, people checked my ID and called the cops to confirm that it wasn't fake. It was annoying and embarrassing each time it happened and made me resent looking so young.

"It's not a bad thing. Just think: when you're in your forties, you'll look like you're still in your thirties."

"Maybe I'd feel differently if I looked older than my age, but it really doesn't bother me that I'm getting older."

"With age comes wisdom."

"Exactly." I take another sip of coffee, then rest it in the cup holder between us. I settle back deeper in my seat and slouch slightly to the side, resting my arm on the console between us and getting more comfortable. "Do you go fishing a lot?"

"Not as often as I'd like to, but I try to go at least once a month to clear my head," he says as I cover my mouth to yawn and try to force my eyes back open. "Sleep, Anna."

"I'm not going to be a very good copilot if I'm sleeping."

"Copilot?"

"When I was learning to drive, my instructor told me being the copilot is just as important as driving the car, because I might see something you don't and then be able to warn you."

"As much as I appreciate that, I think I'll be okay if you sleep for a while." I hear humor in his tone, but I don't have the energy to turn and see if he's smiling. "I'll wake you up when we get to the diner."

I don't ask if he's sure. Between the dim light from the rising sun, the scent of him that's taken over the cab, the warm blanket, and the soft music, I'm lulled to sleep before I can even open my mouth to question him.

"Anna, we're here." My eyes flutter open, and I groan before I sit up and blink against the bright light. I shake out my hand, which has fallen asleep under the weight of my head, and wipe the drool from the corner of my mouth, trying not to make it obvious. "Did you know you snore?"

"I do not," I deny, swinging my head around to narrow my eyes on his.

"You do. It's cute."

"I do not."

"Babe, you do. Hasn't anyone ever told you that?" he asks, sounding curious.

"No, because I don't snore." Or I don't think I do anyway.

"We'll agree to disagree." He smiles, then tips his head to the side questioningly. "Are you hungry?"

"I'm always hungry." I take the blanket off my lap and pick up my bag from the floorboard. Without a word, he gets out, and I start to do the same, but before I can, he opens my door and holds out his hand. I take it and allow him to help me down from my seat. "What's good here?" I ask as we walk hand in hand through the mostly empty parking lot toward the plain-looking restaurant.

"Everything."

"Okay, what's your favorite thing?"

"It's a toss-up between the pancakes and the eggs benedict." He opens the door to the diner for me to walk in ahead of him, and my stomach rumbles as the familiar scent of breakfast food and coffee hits me.

An older woman whose hair is in a long graying braid down her back smiles at us from behind the cash register, where she's ringing up two men. "Grab a couple menus and take a seat anywhere. I'll be with you in a minute," she says.

"Thanks," Calvin says, dipping his chin. He leads me to an empty booth and motions for me to sit before he slides in next to me, leaving the other side empty in a move that makes my chest warm.

"This reminds me of home," I tell him, unwrapping my knife and fork from the napkin.

"Chicago?"

"Yeah," I say quietly, not sure why I called it home when it doesn't feel like it. I'm not sure if it ever did. Not when home is where you should feel the most comfortable, where you can be yourself without worrying about being judged. I never felt like that when I lived in Chicago or when I was around my family or my friends. "In Chicago, there's a diner on almost every corner. I've only seen one since I moved here, and I haven't gone to it yet."

"There are a couple in town, but with tourists come fast food and chain restaurants. There are days I drive down Main Street and don't even recognize it anymore."

"I think most people who grew up in small towns feel that way," I tell him softly. "Everything is becoming modernized, and rural areas are shrinking as cities expand. By the time we have kids and they grow up, small towns won't be so small anymore."

"Do you want kids?"

His question surprises me, and my heart picks up speed. I fiddle with my napkin, unsure how to answer that question. With a deep breath, I decide to be honest. "I like the idea of having kids, but I'm not sure I'd be a good mom. I didn't exactly have a good role model."

"You and your mom weren't close when you were growing up? Did you have anyone else?" he asks curiously.

My throat burns, but I fight against the pain. "No, I had nannies, but they got switched out so often that I learned early to never get attached to them."

"I'm sorry, baby."

"It is what it is." I shrug like it doesn't still hurt, when it does.

"What about your dad?"

"Our relationship was better, but we weren't close," I say, feeling uncomfortable with him for the first time. His parents chose him—they sought him out because they wanted to be parents—while my parents barely seemed to care about my existence until it suited them.

"Sorry about the wait." The woman who greeted us earlier interrupts us with a smile, and I see that the name tag attached to her top says FLO. "Have you two had a chance to look at the menu?" Flo asks, pulling a pen from her pocket while looking at me.

"I'll have coffee and an order of pancakes."

"Just the pancakes, or do you want to add eggs and bacon for a couple bucks more?"

"Can I get my eggs scrambled with cheese?"

"Absolutely, sweetheart." She jots down my order, then looks at Calvin. "What about you, handsome?"

"Same for me."

"Got it." She smiles. "I'll be back in a jiffy with your coffees."

When she's gone, I straighten my silverware, then pick up the little container that has different types of sweetener packets and start organizing them. "Hey." I swing my head around to look at Calvin when he takes it from me. "I was fixing that."

"Why are you nervous?" he asks, with two small creases forming between his brows.

"I'm not nervous," I lie. He takes hold of my hands when I start to tear my napkin into tiny pieces, and I examine the way his hands look holding mine.

"You were fine until I started asking questions about your parents."

"I can see that it might get annoying dating a detective," I mumble to myself, then add quickly and probably too loudly, "not that we're dating."

"I'm getting the urge to kiss you, Anna." My stomach flutters as I get lost in his gaze, and I instinctively lean toward him.

"Coffee," Flo says, and I jump back.

"Thanks," Calvin says, and she nods at him, then winks at me before she walks off.

My cheeks warm, and I attempt to ignore the butterflies in my stomach as I pull my cup of coffee toward me, adding two sugars and some cream. Calvin wraps his arm around my shoulders, then kisses the side of my head as he speaks quietly against my hair. "I won't talk about your parents anymore—not unless you bring them up."

"It's okay," I reply just as quietly, and his lips press to my temple, lingering there for a moment before he picks up his coffee. Keeping his arm around my shoulders, he takes a sip, and I settle into his side, then lift my coffee to blow across the hot liquid. Before I can take a drink, my phone rings, and I pull it out of my pocket. When I see a Chicago number on the screen, I set it facedown on the table.

"Are you going to answer that?"

"Since I don't know who it is, and no one ever calls me from Chicago, I think it's best I don't answer it," I tell him as it stops ringing, only to start up once more.

"It might be important."

"That's doubtful," I say, then push it toward him. "If you're worried, feel free to answer it, but I'm not here," I joke, but my jaw drops when he picks it up and puts it to his ear.

"Hello?" He pauses briefly. "Sorry, she's not available."

I can tell the person on the other end is talking by the faraway look he gets, but it's really annoying that I don't know who it is or what they're saying.

"I'll let her know," he says, and then he makes a growling noise in the back of his throat. "As far as I know, you two are no longer engaged, so it's none of your business who I am to her." He pulls the phone from his ear and tosses it to the table. "I'm thinking you had the right idea 'bout not answering your phone." He jerks his fingers through his hair while glaring at my phone.

"Wa—was that Lance?"

"Yeah, it was Lance." His tone is dry, and he doesn't look at me.

I wait for him to say more, but when he doesn't, I ask, "What did he say?"

"He says you two are still engaged, and he doesn't know why you'd tell people you aren't. Then he asked why the media is calling him and asking about the status of your relationship."

"What?"

"Did you break up with him before you moved here?"

"Yes." I shake my head. "Of course I did. I told him things weren't working, that I wasn't happy, and I gave him back his engagement ring. Then I moved out of the place we shared."

"Well, you'll be able to reiterate that when he comes to see you next week."

I sit back, stunned by the anger in his voice and expression. "He said he's coming?"

"That's what he said." He motions to my phone with a wave of his hand.

"Why is he coming?"

"I don't know, babe. You're going to have to ask him," he says sarcastically, setting my teeth on edge.

I glare at him, then shake my head again. "Actually, that's a great idea." I grab my cell phone and turn it on. When I find Lance's number, I press call and put the phone to my ear, listening to it ring until it goes to voice mail.

"Hi, you've reached Lance. I'm not available, so leave a message."

"Lance, it's me, Anna Belle. Calvin told me you called and seem confused about the status of our relationship, which is odd to me, because we broke up and haven't spoken for . . . I don't know, months. We're over. Hopefully this clarifies things for you." I hang up, slamming down the phone, and then guilt for being so mean hits me. So I pick my phone right back up and go through the whole process of listening to the ringing along with his voice mail message once more. "Sorry, that was rude, but seriously, I don't know why you would think we're still together." I hang up, then groan and call him back again. "Actually, I take that back. I'm not sorry. Also, don't come here; we have no reason to see each other." I don't get the chance to hang up again, because Calvin yanks my phone from my grasp, and he lifts his hips and shoves it in his back pocket. "Hey! That's my phone."

"Yeah, but I have no intention of listening to you call your ex over and over all fucking day."

"I wasn't going to call him again."

"Babe." He scrubs his hands down his face.

"I wasn't."

"You called him three times within the span of three minutes."

I did do that. Damn.

"Why is it that whenever you get pissed at me, I haven't gotten an apology?" he asks, and I notice the anger has left his features and that his lips are twitching.

"Probably because you were being a jerk and I wasn't sorry," I tell him honestly.

He grins like he thinks I'm cute, but then his smile falters. "I'm guessing, since he's getting calls, Max published the story."

"Yeah." I let out a long breath and pick up my coffee to take a sip as I wonder what she wrote in the story.

"Good news is, out on the lake, there's no cell service, so you'll have a little peace," he tells me, his expression gentling.

"Bad news is," I say, my nose scrunching, "if I see Max again, I'm probably going to kick her in the shin, so you might have to arrest me."

"I don't know. I kinda like the idea of you wearing my cuffs." He smirks, and my insides somersault.

"Breakfast is served," Flo singsongs, setting down two overflowing plates. "I'm going to come back with syrup, but is there anything else you want?" She looks between the two of us.

"I'm good," Calvin says.

"Ketchup for me, please." I smile as the smell of bacon and pancakes urges me to dig in.

"Got it. I'll be right back."

I pick up a piece of bacon when she walks off and take a bite, trying not to moan in happiness. I never buy real bacon; I always get turkey bacon because it's supposed to be better for me, but no matter what the packaging says, it's just not the same. After the waitress comes back and drops off the syrup and ketchup, we dig into our food.

"I think this is the best breakfast I've had in forever," I tell Calvin while dipping a bite of eggs and cheese into some ketchup.

He turns to smile at me. "I wouldn't have guessed, based on the sounds you're making."

"I'm not making any sounds."

"You're moaning every time you take a bite."

"Whatever." I don't even bother arguing with him. Instead, I enjoy my cheesy eggs, take another bite of pancake, and wash it all down with some coffee.

When we're done eating and are stuffed, he pays the bill, and we load back up in his truck. "The lake is only about twenty minutes from here. We'll stop at the tackle shop, pick you up a license, and get the keys for the boat," he says as we pull onto the highway.

Wait, what?

"License? A license for what?"

"You have to have a license to fish."

"Do I need to take a test?" I ask, getting that same nervousness I used to feel when I had to take a test in school.

He laughs like I'm being funny. "No test."

I sigh in relief, then ask, "We're going out on a boat?"

"Yeah, not a big one, just a skiff, so we can get out into deeper water and away from the shore, which I'm sure will be crowded."

"Cool," I say absently, looking out the window and soaking in the beauty of the area as we eventually get off the highway and turn onto an old gravel road. There are a few houses tucked back in the woods, but it's mostly trees as far as the eye can see.

He takes my hand as we crest the top of a small hill, and a lake so still it looks like glass comes into view. "This is where I want to retire one day."

"I can see why. It's absolutely beautiful."

"Yeah." He places his hand on my lap and follows the road around the edge of the lake. We reach an area with a few cabins lined up side by side, and he parks in front of one with a hand-painted wooden sign hanging over the door, proclaiming the place THE SHACK.

"Grab your ID from your bag, babe. You'll need it for the paperwork you have to fill out."

I dig into my purse for my ID as he gets out, and by the time I find it, he has my door open and has reached around to unbuckle me. "I know you're very excited about fishing." I turn in my seat so my legs are hanging out the door. "But I am fully capable of unhooking myself and getting out of your truck."

Without a word, he wraps his hand around the back of my neck and pulls me forward, covering my mouth with his. Tingles shoot up my spine, and I lean into him, placing my hands on his shoulders as the tip of his tongue touches my lips. I open, the kiss deepens, and his hands wander up my thighs and to my sides. The urge to wrap my legs around his hips and grind against him causes a whimper of need to escape my throat, and his arms wrap tight around me.

Before I'm ready for the kiss to end, he tears his mouth from mine, slides his fingers into my hair to cup the back of my head, and tucks my face into his neck, muttering a quiet "Fuck."

"Was that a 'shut up' kiss?" I pull back to look at him, still breathing heavily and dazed from the kiss.

"No, that was an 'I've been wanting to kiss you all morning but never had the opportunity to kiss you until now' kiss."

"Good to know." I lick my lips. "I like that kiss way more than the 'shut up' kiss."

His eyes heat up as they drop to my mouth. "We should get this done so we can get out on the lake."

"If you move, I'll get down and we can get on with that."

"Give me a minute, sweetheart."

My brows drag together. "I thought you were ready to go in."

"Yeah, but I'm not really down with everyone seeing how badly I want you." My lips part as his hips tilt slightly into mine, showing me exactly what he means. "Yeah," he mutters, and I smile, a little proud of myself for causing that kind of reaction. "Your cute, pleased little smile isn't helping matters."

"I'm not doing anything."

"You're breathing, babe."

"Do you want me to hold my breath?" I ask, and his eyes narrow slightly. "What? I'm just trying to help."

"Just be quiet."

"Okay." I pretend to zip my lips closed and toss the key away.

"Stop being fucking cute."

"I'm not doing anything!" I start to laugh.

"Yeah, you are."

"Fine, just pretend I'm not here." I press my lips together and sit completely still.

"Fuck it. This is obviously not going to go away anytime soon." He pulls me down from the cab and sets me on my feet. "Just stand in front of me."

"Sure," I say with a laugh. He slams the door shut, and I start to walk with him right behind me, his hand wrapped around the side of my waist. "I feel like we look like you're holding me at gunpoint or something," I whisper as we walk up the steps to the porch.

"It'll be fine." He raises his hand over the top of my shoulder and opens a wooden screen door with a metal handle attached to it. I step inside, and it takes a moment for my eyes to adjust to the light. When they do, I see the room is set up like a small convenience store, with aisles of food and fishing supplies.

"How can I help you two?" a man wearing denim overalls and an old blue baseball cap over his white hair asks from behind the counter.

"She needs a fishing license, and I reserved a skiff for today under the name Miller."

The man nods and grabs a clipboard from the wall behind him. "I'll need to see your ID, honey." I walk to the counter and hand over my license. Once he's done copying my information, he hands the ID back to me, along with the clipboard. "Fill in the blanks," he instructs, then looks to Calvin. "While she's working on that, you can follow me out to the dock. We'll check the boat over and make sure everything's in working order."

"Sounds good," Calvin agrees, giving my waist a squeeze. "Be right back."

"I'll be here," I say, and he leans in to touch his mouth to mine, then looks over the top of my head, lifting his chin to signal he's ready to go. When the two of them leave, I quickly fill out the rest of the paperwork; then, like most women who are left alone in a store, I end up distracted by the stuff on the shelves. I grab a basket from beside the door and pick up chips, cookies, and candy bars, then go to the cooler on the back wall and take out a few bottles of water, ignoring the Styrofoam containers labeled **WORMS**.

I carry my overflowing basket to the register and set it down, then walk down the aisle of poles and pick up a pink one. It's cute and sparkly—totally me. I take it back to the counter with me and place it next to my other items, then turn to watch Calvin open the door and come toward me, with the old man following him.

"I got us some snacks," I say, and he drops his gaze to the basket, then looks at me, raising a brow. "Okay, a lot of snacks." I grin, and his eyes move over my face before landing on my mouth.

His lips tip into a smile, and he shakes his head, then looks over the top of my head. "How much do I owe you, Bruce?"

I turn to look at the man who must be Bruce and watch him sign the bottom of my paperwork. He adds up my stuff, and when he gets to the fishing pole, he picks it up and grins like an idiot. "You've got good taste, girl."

"Thanks." I grin back.

"That'll be forty for the license, twenty-six for the junk, and two fifty-two for the pole," he replies, and my mouth drops open.

"Are you saying that fishing pole costs over two hundred dollars?" I squeak as Calvin starts to pull out his wallet.

"It's a good one," Bruce informs me.

That might be, but still. "It's just a fishing pole."

"It's one of the best on the market, and it's pink."

"It's fine." Calvin starts to hand over his credit card, but I cover his hand with mine, then very carefully take the pole from Bruce.

"Even though I'm sure this pole has some kind of magical fishing powers, I'm going to pass up getting it today," I tell him, and then I pull out the eighty dollars in cash I have in my pocket and hand it over to Bruce. "That's for my license and the food."

"Anna." There's a slight tinge of annoyance in Calvin's voice, but I don't look at him.

"I'll just put this up." I carry the pole back to where I got it from, then meet Calvin at the door. When I reach his side, he hands me back my cash, and I frown.

"I'm paying for your license and the food, and we're not going to argue about it."

"Yo—" I start to tell him that he's annoying, but before I even get the first word out, he kisses me swiftly, cutting me off.

"Let's go." He holds the door open for me to step out ahead of him, but I don't move.

I cross my arms over my chest and narrow my eyes when his gaze drops to my lips. "Don't think you can just kiss me anytime you want to keep me quiet."

"Why not? It works."

I growl in the back of my throat, and he chuckles as he takes my hand.

"Come on, sweetheart. I'd like to get on the lake before the fish quit biting," he urges, but I raise a brow and tap my foot. "And I won't kiss you anymore to keep you quiet."

"Thank you." I step out onto the porch, then look for the truck.

"I parked around back." He leads me around the side of the cabin to a big dirt lot. "Do you want your bag?"

"No, but I need my sunglasses and sunscreen," I tell him, and he pulls out his keys and hands them to me. I go to the passenger door while he goes to the back, and once I have my sunglasses on, I grab my sunscreen and shove it in my pocket. By the time I get to the back of the truck, he has a cooler, a tackle box, and two fishing poles on the open tailgate.

"Did either of these cost two hundred dollars?" I ask, picking up the poles as he shoves the bag of junk food and water into the cooler I didn't know he had.

"More." He takes the handle of the cooler in one hand and the tackle box in the other, then looks at me. "Ready?"

"Yep."

I walk at his side across the lot and onto a wooden dock. When we reach the end, he stops at a small metal boat that has a single engine attached to the back. "I'm gonna get in first; then I'll help you in," he explains.

I watch him easily step down into the boat, still holding both his items, and once he's set them down, he takes the poles from me and holds out his hand.

"Maybe I should sit down on the edge and scoot in," I suggest as I look at his hand, then the boat, which is rocking from side to side.

"Or you could trust me."

"Trust you." I lick my lips. "Right, I can totally do that." I grasp his hand and step down onto the seat. The boat sways under my weight, and I scream before latching onto him and wrapping both my arms around his waist. When I register that the boat is no longer moving but his body is shaking, I peel my eyes open and tip my head back. "Are you laughing at me?"

"No," he lies, grasping my hands from behind his back and bringing them between us. "I'm gonna help you down, and then, once you're seated, I'll unhook us from the dock. Do you want a life jacket?"

"No, I can swim," I say, shuddering at the memory of my recent experience, and he lifts my hands and kisses my white knuckles. I sit and grasp onto the metal under me and use my weight to help keep us balanced as he unties us and steps over my seat to start the engine.

"Come over here." He holds out his hand, and I bite my lip as I take it, then slowly make my way to where he's straddling the bench near the engine. I sit between his spread legs with my back to his front, and he wraps one arm around my middle, keeping me tight against him as he pulls back on the throttle, causing the boat to begin speeding through the water. "See? It's not so scary."

"It's actually kind of nice." I relax into him with a smile on my face as he drives us across the lake toward a small island with a handful of trees sticking out of it.

When we reach the edge, he circles around to the far side of the island and shuts down the engine. "I'm going to set up our poles."

"What can I do to help?"

"Nothing yet." He moves away from me, and I look over the edge into the dark water but don't see any fish close to the surface, and then I tip my head back toward the sky and the sun, which is high above us now. Knowing how quickly I'll burn if I don't have on sunblock, I take the tube I brought with me from my pocket, then slip off my hoodie and start applying it. Once I'm done, I focus on what Calvin is doing and become instantly entranced as I watch him work.

No other guy I've dated has been what you would call "outdoorsy," and I wouldn't have trusted any of them to take care of me if we'd gotten stranded on the side of the road with a flat tire. But I'm starting to see Calvin is nothing like any guy I've ever known. He's not some hipster pretending to be all manly because it's cool, and that is a serious turn-on.

"You okay?"

I lift my eyes off his hands, which are hooking a fuzzy, bright-colored lure to the line, and meet his gaze. "I really want to kiss you right now." I hold his stare, then my breath, as he gets up and looms over me.

"I'm good with you kissing me anytime you get that urge."

"Good to know," I breathe, leaning up to press my mouth to his as he bends toward me.

The kiss is deep and wet and over far too quickly. When he pulls away, I have the desire to drag him back for more. I start to do just that, but the boat rocks, scaring me.

"I'm definitely good with you wanting to kiss me," I tell him, and he grins as I gasp in surprise as the boat rocks again. "That said, I think we should wait until we're on solid ground."

"Good idea," he murmurs, making me laugh, and he smiles, then holds out his hand.

"You want me to stand up?"

"I'm going to teach you to cast. It's easier if you're standing."

I stand up and watch him go through the steps of casting out the line, then take the pole and try myself.

"I did it!" I fight the urge to jump around when I get it right on the first try.

"Good job, baby."

"Now what?" I watch the bobber a few feet from the boat, floating on top of the water.

"Now, you wait." He kisses the side of my head, then grabs his pole and casts out his line.

"Why don't you have one of the bobber things on yours?"

"I don't need it." He takes a seat next to me. "After I bring you out here a few times, you won't need one either."

I look around at the beauty surrounding us, feeling his leg and arm pressed against mine, and even though I'm enjoying this moment, I'm looking forward to more days spent just like this with the man sitting next to me.

Suggestion 8

Don't Believe What You Hear

CALVIN

I look over the crime scene photos on my desk, trying to figure out what I'm missing. The place where I grew up has had its fair share of crime, and there have been more than a few murders in the area over the years. But none of them have gone cold as quickly as the two cases that have recently hit my desk.

I pick up the photo of Chris Davis, a student from Ohio who was here with his girlfriend and a few of their college friends on vacation. His body was found near the beach, with lacerations around his wrists and neck, but no rope was found in the area, meaning whoever committed the crime had taken it with them when they left. His girlfriend and friends said they had been out the night before, partying at the clubs in the area, and around two in the morning, he told his girlfriend he was going outside to smoke but never returned. No other physical evidence was left at the crime scene due to the rain that had fallen the morning his body was found by a woman walking her dog. The surveillance cameras in the area never caught a clear picture of him, and no one witnessed him coming or going from the club.

I drop Chris's photo and pick up the one of Mike Hurl, a bartender whose body was found last night by a runner in one of the local parks. Where Chris died of strangulation, Mike died from blunt-force trauma to the back of his skull, and the weapon—a hammer—was left at the scene. I drop Mike's photo and look at both men side by side. Both of them were around the same age, attractive, and fit, and both were murdered in the last month. The two cases have nothing else in common, but still my gut is telling me they're linked. I just don't know how.

With a groan of frustration, I sit back in my chair and scrub my hands down my face. There's nothing worse than having an open case, especially when loved ones are looking to you for answers you can't give.

"Cal, you good, man?"

I look at Herb, sitting a desk away. A man who took me under his wing when I was a rookie and taught me everything he knew about being a detective.

"Yeah, I just need coffee and some air." I stand, pick up my badge, and clip it to my belt before holstering my gun on my hip.

"Maybe you should go home to shower," he suggests, informing me without actually saying the words that I look like shit.

Last evening, two seconds after I'd pulled up to Anna's place, Herb called to tell me that I was needed. So instead of spending the night with Anna, like I hoped I'd be doing, I spent the night at a crime scene and then the morning talking to Mike's friends and neighbors, looking for leads.

"I might stop by my house to shower, but I'll be back. The medical examiner should be calling this afternoon, and I want to be around to meet with him."

"Right," he mutters. "I'll see you back here in a few hours then. And you should know my kids are refusing to let me bring your dog back to you, so you're gonna have to live without him for another few days."

"Understood." I smile as I pick up my cell and shove it in my pocket. "You know you could just get them a dog of their own."

"No, thanks. I'll just borrow yours. That way I can give him back," he says.

I laugh. "I'll be back."

"See ya." He gives me a salute, and I lift my chin.

After I get to my truck, I head across town to the Sweet Spot, figuring I'll kill two birds with one stone by getting some coffee and my fix of Anna. I park down the block from the bakery, and noticing a crowd gathered at the door, I bypass everyone, ignoring the comments and grumbles, and head inside. The place is packed: every table is taken up with customers, and there's a line of people waiting for their turn. I spot Chrissie at the register and can tell by her expression that she's annoyed by whatever the woman in front of her is saying.

"Please tell me that you're here to help."

I look to my right and find Gaston clearing off a table. "What the hell is going on?"

"Your woman is popular, and everyone and their mother is here trying to get a glimpse of the millionaire girl who works at the local bakery."

"Jesus." I look around, noting then that most of the customers have the same look on their faces people get when they're passing by the scene of an accident, like they're trying to get a peek at the carnage that's been left behind.

"They want her to sign their papers, take a photo, or both." He shakes his head. "I don't get it, but they all seem to think she's famous. Especially after her ex talked to the media and said he loves her, has been giving her time to find herself, and that he's waiting for her to come home so they can finish planning their wedding and start their life together."

"She's not marrying him," I say with more force than necessary.

"I know that, big guy, but that's what he's saying, and the media is eating it up."

Right, the fucking dick. The fact that he didn't come here the moment she took off and drag her ass back home proves how big of an idiot he is.

"Hey, Calvin." Chrissie gives me a tired smile as I follow Gaston around the back of the counter.

"You doin' okay, babe?" Gaston asks her, stopping to kiss the side of her head.

"I'm fine." She pats his cheek, then looks at me. "Anna's in the back."

"Is she coming out here?" the woman at the front of the line asks, sounding anxious, and I turn to face her. "I'd like her to sign my paper." She sets it faceup on the counter, and I see a photo of Anna wearing a formfitting dress under the arm of a good-looking man with a smug smile who's wearing a tux. The headline reads COLD FEET OR COLD HEARTED?

"Like I told you before, ma'am, she's not coming out."

"Why not?" She plants her hands on her wide hips. "I drove over an hour just to see her."

"And you can drive an hour back home," I tell her, placing my hand on my waist near my badge, and her eyes widen when they drop to it. "Enjoy your cookies and your day."

Her nose scrunches, and she grumbles something under her breath, then turns to walk away.

"Thanks." Chrissie shakes her head, smiling at the next customer in line while holding up her finger in a "just a moment" gesture. "Most of the people have been cool about not seeing her, but a few like her have been persistent."

"Is she okay?" I glance at the doorway that leads to the kitchen, and even though I know she's back there, she isn't visible.

"She's annoyed by the attention, but she's all right. I'm sure she'd be happy to see you."

"Are you good with me going back there?"

"Of course," she says brightly, and I see her husband roll his eyes.

"Thanks." I head through the open door and stop to watch Anna beating a rolling pin into a large lump of dough on a metal table. "That bad?"

She jumps at my question and spins around to face me. I notice then that she's been crying. "Hey, how did everything go with work last night?" she asks, wiping the tears off her cheeks with the sleeve of her shirt.

"Why are you crying?"

"I'm not." She drops her hands to her sides. "It's just the flour making my allergies act up."

"Are people actually allergic to flour?"

"Yes, haven't you heard of gluten allergies?"

I smile; I can't help it. "It must be hard on you, working in a bakery and being allergic to flour, then."

She shrugs, and I close the distance between us and hold out my arms.

She looks unsure for a moment, but then her face crumples and she drops her forehead to my chest, wrapping her arms around me and holding on tight. "Lance went on the news last night and made it seem like I just needed a break but we were still together." She tips her head back to meet my gaze. "Can you believe that?"

"Yes," I say easily, even though I don't like the idea of him laying claim to her. "He's probably realizing he was an idiot for letting you go."

I swipe the last bit of wetness from her cheeks, and her expression softens; then her nose scrunches adorably. "I'm not going back to Chicago, and I'm not getting back with him."

"Are you trying to convince me or yourself?"

"Do I need to convince you?" she asks, studying me, and I shake my head. "Then I'm just saying it out loud."

Good to know. I'm not sure how I'd deal if she told me she was having second thoughts about her ex. "Have you talked to him today?"

"No, but he's called, and so have my parents and a few of my friends." She steps back and lets out a deep breath. "I don't know what to do. I never thought I'd be dealing with this kind of situation, and now Chrissie is dealing with it too."

"I don't think she's upset about having paying customers."

"The shop doesn't need my drama." She leans against the table behind her.

"I won't be happy if you use this as an excuse to run off," I warn her.

She sighs. "All I'm saying is I don't know what to do to put an end to this mess."

"Maybe you should make a statement to the press." That comment comes from the doorway, and we both look at Gaston as he walks into the kitchen. "I'll reiterate what Calvin said and tell you now that I'll be pissed—and Chrissie will too—if you up and leave. That said, I get why this situation is stressful. But I think if you make it clear publicly that you're not going back to your old life and that you are happy where you are, people will leave it alone, including your ex."

"I'm not going to run away. I wouldn't do that to Chrissie," Anna says quietly, holding Gaston's stare. "And I'm not going to go to the media. I know that would only fan the flames and, in the end, create more problems."

"So what's your plan?" I ask.

"I need to talk to Lance." She chews the inside of her cheek. "I don't know why he's doing this now, but I need to make him understand he needs to stop and that there is no chance of us getting back together."

"My guess is he's doing all of this to save face. Right now," I say, and she looks away. "It's not about you; it's about protecting his image. That's why he spoke to the media about you two."

"He's right, Anna," Gaston agrees, picking up a metal sheet pan with rows of cookies off a rack and heading toward the door with it. "Whatever you decide to do, you know we all have your back."

"Thanks."

"Anytime." He gives her a smile, then disappears.

When he's gone, she focuses on me and eyes me from head to toe as she frowns. "Have you been home since you dropped me off last night?"

"No, I was heading that way but stopped to see you first."

Her eyes warm and her voice is soft when she asks, "Did you eat lunch?"

"I'm not hungry."

I see the understanding in her gaze. "Do you want some coffee, then?"

"If it means you going out front, no. I'll stop and pick some up on the way home."

She nods. "Are you working tonight?"

"I have two open cases on my desk right now. Until I close them, I'll be working."

"I understand." She doesn't try to hide the disappointment in her voice.

"I still gotta eat and wouldn't mind your company while doing that."

"Okay."

"I have to go back to work this afternoon for a few hours, but I should be home by the time you get off work. How about you come to my place, and I'll cook dinner?"

"Or I can make something. I'm sure the last thing you want to do after being up all day is cook."

"Can you cook?"

"I think so. I guess you'll find out." She smiles.

I take a step toward her, then lean in and touch my lips to hers. "You gonna be okay here?"

"Yeah." She waves off my concern. "This too shall pass."

"All right, I'll see you tonight."

"I'll see you tonight," she whispers against my lips as I kiss her once more. When I step away, I grin at the dazed look on her face, and she rolls her eyes, making me laugh.

I head out to the front of the shop and stop next to Chrissie and Gaston at the register before pulling out one of my cards and handing it to Gaston. "If things get out of hand here, just call, and I'll come with a few of my men to clear the crowd."

"Thanks, man." He reaches his hand out to mine, and we shake once.

"Later."

"Yeah, later." Chrissie gives me a smile, and Gaston dips his chin.

I leave the shop and stop in my tracks when I see a newsstand down the block from the bakery with three shelves filled with the local paper. I buy them all, then toss all but one into a recycling bin on the way out, ignoring the looks I get.

Once in my truck, I open the paper and get stuck on the look in Anna's eyes, a look that states very clearly she was uncomfortable. Not that the man next to her seemed to notice, or maybe he didn't care. I throw the paper into the passenger seat, not even bothering to scan the story. Before I can drive off, my phone rings, and my mom's name flashes on the screen.

"Mom," I answer as I pull out into traffic.

"Calvin," she says, sounding worried or nervous. I can't tell which.

"Is everything okay?" I ask her when she doesn't say more.

"Oh . . . I don't know how to tell you this, especially after you spent yesterday with Anna."

I frown. "What?"

"Anna, honey. I just heard she's engaged and getting back with her ex."

"She's not getting back with her ex, Mom," I say with a sigh. I should have known she'd hear about this latest drama and buy into the bullshit, like everyone else has.

"She is, Calvin. It was in the paper, and Jana said she even heard about the story on some podcast she listens to."

"Jana, whoever she is, doesn't know what she's talking about. I just left Anna at the bakery, and she's coming to my place tonight for dinner."

"What?"

"I don't have the time to explain this right now, Mom. All I can tell you is don't believe what you read, and please don't listen to what anyone is saying."

"Are you sure, Calvin? The story said she's here in town because she got cold feet and needed time to sort out her head."

"She didn't get cold feet. She wasn't happy with him and ended things."

"Why on earth would he lie?" She sounds flabbergasted.

"Why the fuck did he let her go in the first place, Mom? My guess is the guy's an idiot."

"Is . . . is Anna okay?"

"She's upset this is all playing out in the media, but otherwise she's fine," I assure her.

"And you two are still seeing each other?"

"Yeah, we're still seeing each other." I smile as I turn onto my street.

"I didn't believe what I heard, but then I saw the paper, and after what happened with you and Vickie—"

"It's all good, Mom." I cut her off, not wanting her to bring up my ex, not when I haven't even thought about her for a while. There was a time when what had happened between us played over and over in my mind almost daily. I used to wonder if we would still be together if I had done some things differently. Now I know we just weren't meant to be. "I just got home, so I'm gonna shower before I head back to the station. I'll call you tomorrow."

"Well, okay. Love you, and tell Anna I said hi and that she can stop by the house anytime. She's always welcome."

I laugh. "I'll let her know. Later, Mom."

"Bye, honey." She hangs up, and I drop my cell into the cup holder. I hope Anna is strong enough to deal with this mess, and if she's not, I hope that she trusts me to be there for her. This town is small, and most people believe what they hear, so I know it won't be easy on her.

I shut down the engine of my truck, then get out and walk to the end of my driveway, lifting my chin to Sandy when she drives by waving. I grab the mail and sort through it as I head inside, then add a few bills to an ever-growing pile on the dining table before I carry the junk to the kitchen trash can. Knowing Anna will be here tonight, I pick up the kitchen and living room, and then I change the sheets on my bed and throw some laundry into the washer before I hop in the shower.

Dressed and drinking a cup of coffee an hour later, I pick up my cell when the number for the morgue pops up.

"Yeah."

"Calvin, it's Frank." It's the lead medical examiner. "I just finished with the autopsy."

"Please tell me you have something for me."

"Maybe. You got time to stop by here?"

"Yep, give me thirty."

"See you then." He hangs up, and I down the rest of my coffee before heading out, calling Herb on the way to let him know to meet me.

∾

"So we got nothing," Herb says as we step out of the building where the medical examiner's office is located.

"We have something." I inhale a breath of fresh air, trying to get rid of the stench of death and embalming fluid that's filled my senses for the last thirty minutes. "He found hair, and skin under the victim's nails. And now we know he was dead less than three hours before his body was found."

"We need a suspect to match those hairs to, and his neighbors and friends said he hooked up with women and men at random and didn't keep anyone updated on where he was going or what he was doing. Right now, we're still at square one."

Fuck, I hate that he's right. "So what now?" I ask, hoping he has an idea for a new direction.

"You should go home, get some rest, and hit the ground running tomorrow." He holds up his hand when I start to argue with him. "You haven't slept, and you won't be of any use to me or anyone else if you pass out from exhaustion. I'm going to go back to the station and make a few calls." I run my fingers through my hair, then sigh. "If I find anything out, I'll call you." He pats my arm. "Get some rest, man. Tomorrow is a new day." I know he's right. I'm running on fumes at this point. Still, I hate leaving things undone, especially when the victims' families won't rest until we give them some closure.

"Yeah." I let out a breath, then head for my truck across the lot, and once I'm inside, I pull out my cell and send Anna a text with directions to my place. I start up the engine, and a second later my phone buzzes. Even with the shit weighing heavily on my mind, I smile as I picture the annoyed look she often gets as I read her text.

I tried to go to the store to pick up something to make for dinner, but after the third person stopped me and asked if I was the girl in the paper, I left. I hope you like grilled cheese and tomato soup, because that's all I have at home.

I pat my phone against my thigh, wondering if asking her to stay the night with me would be pushing things too fast. From all the signs she's given me, she's in as deep as I am. I dial her number, hoping I'm not wrong.

"Hey," she answers, sounding as tired as I feel.

"Leave the grilled cheese and soup. Just bring yourself and pajamas," I say as I stop at a red light.

"What?"

"I'm fucking exhausted. We're ordering in Chinese and hanging out in my bed, watching movies."

"You know . . ." I hear a smile in her voice as she continues speaking. "I should argue and say I'm not going to hang out in bed with you."

I grin. "You should, but are you going to?"

"No." She lets out a long breath. "That actually sounds like the best idea I've heard all day."

"Good, I'll be home in twenty." I flip on the signal to turn into the parking lot for the liquor store, where I plan on grabbing a bottle of wine and a case of beer.

"I'll be over after I get my stuff together."

"See you soon, baby."

"See you soon." She hangs up, and even with the shit swirling in my head, I'm looking forward to going home.

Suggestion 9

WELCOME THE UNEXPECTED

ANNA

"Anna!" Edie shouts through the door as I shove a pair of comfortable pajamas and clothes for tomorrow into the overnight bag on my bed.

"It's open! Come on in," I shout back.

"Where on earth do you think you're going?" she asks angrily, and my eyes fly up just in time to see her plant herself in front of the door and cross her arms over her chest. "You are not running away just because that idiot ex of yours is making a damn fool of himself."

"I'm not running away." I shake my head, wondering why everyone thinks I will. "I'm going to Calvin's."

"You're packing a bag to go to Calvin's?" She looks around like she's trying to see if I've packed anything else.

"Yeah."

"Are you staying the night with him?"

"Maybe." I grab my sneakers and put them in the side compartment of my bag. "He didn't say, but I want to make sure I have stuff with me for the morning in case I do."

"Oh." She uncrosses her arms and walks toward the bed.

"Did you need something?"

"You haven't changed this place since you moved in."

I glance around and shrug. "I changed up the bathroom."

"Okay, but everything else is the same. Nothing says this is your home."

She's right. I haven't really made the space mine. It still looks like a hotel, if I'm honest.

"I still need to plan a trip back to Chicago to get all my stuff. I just haven't had time to do it. Maybe after Chrissie has the baby, I'll take a weekend." I shrug, then add, "Or maybe I'll just give up my storage unit and get new stuff. There's nothing in it that really means anything to me."

"I'd go with you to Chicago." My chest warms at her offer. "Though if I saw that ex of yours, I'd probably hurt him, so it might be best if I stay put," she says, and I laugh.

"I don't know. I kinda want to hurt him for the mess he's caused." My lip curls. "Well, him and that woman, Max, who started this all."

Her expression softens at the mention of Max. "You're really okay?"

"I'm really okay, and I'm not going to run away. Promise."

"I would drag you back here if you did."

My throat gets oddly tight, and I have to force myself to swallow over the lump that's formed. Three times today, people have told me they would be upset if I left. Not one person seemed to really care when I was leaving Chicago, and those were people I'd known my whole life—or most of it anyway. "I know you would."

She nods and looks away, like she's uncomfortable. "Now, about you and Calvin."

"Edie," I groan.

"What? I just want to tell you that I'm happy for you. He's a good man."

"I'm starting to see that," I agree, thinking that's an understatement.

"Now, I'll let you get going. I'm sure you're anxious to spend some time with him."

"Nah." I wave her off, and she raises a brow. "Is it that obvious?"

"It's written all over your face," she tells me with a smirk. I don't know how I feel about my emotions being so easily read.

"Maybe I should play a little hard to get."

"Or maybe you should just keep doing what you're doing, because it's working," she suggests.

"You're probably right."

"I have years of experience dealing with men. Trust me, I'm right." She winks before turning and placing her hand on the handle of the door. "I'll see you tomorrow evening."

"See you tomorrow." I watch her leave, then head into my bathroom to grab my makeup remover, my toothbrush, and a few other things I'll need if I spend the night. Then, after I shove it all in my bag, I take it out to my car and head to Calvin's.

When my GPS lets me know I've arrived, I smile as I turn into his driveway and park behind his truck. His house is adorable, with deep-blue vinyl siding, white shutters on either side of each window, and a white picket fence encompassing the front yard. I get out, taking my purse and overnight bag with me, and before I even get to the gate leading to the walk, the front door opens, and Calvin—wearing jeans, a plain black tee, and bare feet—steps outside and walks down the path to greet me.

"I love your house." I grin at him as he reaches over to unlock and open the gate for me.

"Don't get too excited. It's a mess inside." He leans in to kiss me, taking my bag with him as he leans back. "Most of the work I've done has been out here. The inside is a work in progress."

"It's cute. I love the picket fence."

"When I bought the place, the fence was mostly rotted away and falling down, and I planned on ripping it all out, but Mom convinced me to keep it. I haven't decided if it's worth the effort of having it, since I gotta paint it every summer."

"Well, I think it's perfect," I say as he opens the front door. The moment I step inside, I see why he said it's a work in progress. The wood floors need to be refinished and the walls need paint, but I can see it's got character, and when it's done, it will be gorgeous. "Where's Bane?"

"My partner's kids kidnapped him. I'll get him back in a few days. I just have to wait until he chews up something of theirs and they stop thinking he's cute."

I laugh. "You might be waiting awhile, then."

"Maybe," he agrees. Then he asks, "Do you want a tour of my house?"

"Yes."

"Good thing I picked up earlier." He grins and takes my hand. He leads me a little ways down the hall to an open door, and when he flips on the light, I see a beautiful bedroom with beige walls and plush carpeting. There's a dark wooden king-size bed in the center of the room, matching nightstands on either side, and a dresser against the wall near the door. I step into the room as he places my bag on the end of the bed, and I notice that the photo of a lake surrounded by deep-green trees above the bed matches the comforter and pillows perfectly.

"I've only finished this room and the master bath," he tells me, taking my purse and tossing it on the bed before grabbing my hand and leading me across the room to a closed door. When he opens it, I see it's nothing like the overly modern design I'm used to. I also see he's taken time picking out each item carefully. The dark-brown wood-looking tile on the floor continues up the walls, making it feel cave-like, and the glass-enclosed shower with a stone floor is big enough for four people. Two sinks sit on a single wall-mounted wooden stand, and the mirrors above each one glow around the edges. Cool antique-looking faucets match the light fixtures on either side of the mirrors.

"Did you do this yourself?"

"My dad, my brother, and I did all the tile work. I paid someone to finish out the shower and hang all the fixtures."

"It feels like a cave." I step into the room and run my hand along the edge of one of the sinks.

"That's what I was going for. I wanted it to feel like the outdoors indoors."

"You pulled it off." I walk toward him when he holds out his hand.

He smiles, shuts off the light, and leads me back into the hall. He opens another door to a room that's stuffed full with cans of paint, ladders, and everything else needed to fix up a house. "This will at some point be another bedroom." He closes the door, then leads me to another room, this one with a beat-up desk and an older computer and chair along with a few paper clippings framed on the wall. "My office." He shuts the door, then taps another one but doesn't open it. "Guest bath." He continues walking and stops at an open doorway, through which there's a large living room with a fireplace, an old couch with a missing cushion, and a TV on what looks like a side table.

"I'm starting in here next," he says as he leads me into a kitchen that's in major need of repair. The appliances are old, and the cabinets and counters are peeling. "Through that arch"—he points at the opening on one side of the room—"is the dining room, but I plan on tearing down the wall and making this all one space with an island and a breakfast nook."

"I love it," I reply, hoping I don't sound like I'm designing the space in my head, even though that is totally what I'm doing. "Does that door lead to the backyard?" I ask, motioning to the door at the end of the counter.

"Yeah." He opens it, and I look out at the backyard, which is surprisingly large and is fully enclosed with a tall wooden fence.

"Nice." I look up at him and gasp when his mouth suddenly lands on mine and his fingers slide into my hair. I latch onto his shirt with both hands and tip my head to the side as he deepens the kiss. His hand curves around my back, and I arch into him, my breasts pressing against his chest. He growls against my tongue, sending a tingle down my spine. When his mouth leaves mine, I'm breathless and dazed. My eyes flutter open to meet his, and I see the same desire I feel reflected back at me. "Is that normal?"

"What?" he asks, sliding his hand around to cup my jaw and sweep his thumb over my bottom lip.

"This kind of overwhelming need I feel when it comes to you."

"I'm not sure if it's normal, but I feel it too." His thumb caresses my lips again. "From the moment I saw you, I felt it."

"You weren't very nice to me the first time we met," I remind him, resting my hands flat against his chest.

"Yeah," he agrees, looking a little guilty.

"You're lucky you're handsome, Detective Miller." I pat his chest, and he laughs as he captures my hand and kisses it.

"I did apologize," he reminds me.

"Because your mom told you to," I say; then I laugh at the look of surprise on his face. "She mentioned it the day of the barbecue."

"I would've done it anyway."

I raise a brow at him.

"I would have, and it doesn't matter; you're here now."

"I am," I reply, and he slides his arms around me, tugging me closer.

"I like you here."

"Do you?"

"Oh yeah." His lips press to mine, and I move my hands up to his shoulders and then freeze when his cell rings. "Shit," he groans, and my stomach sinks. "While I get that, why don't you go change?"

I nod, and he kisses the tip of my nose, then lets me go. I leave the kitchen and hear him answer the phone behind me with a brisk "Yeah," but I don't stick around to hear what else he says. I head down the hall-way to his room and go in, closing the door behind me. I change into my sleep pants and T-shirt, then fold the clothes I had on and put them back into my bag. Once I'm done, I place the bag on the floor and go to the door. Since he's still on the phone, I give him some time to finish his call. I grab my cell from my purse and open my texts. I see that not only has Lance messaged, but so have my dad and Lucy.

I fight back a groan of frustration when I see Lance has sent me his flight itinerary for the upcoming weekend, along with the information for the hotel where he's staying. I send him a text, asking him to please not come, and then open the message from my dad. I take a seat on the end of Calvin's bed as I read it.

> We've put up with this foolishness long enough, Anna. It's time for you to come home. Call me.

I text him back with shaking fingers.

> I'm not a child having a tantrum, and I am home. I wish you could be happy for me and support me.

My thumb hovers over the send button for a moment before I press it. Whatever my parents' deal is, I no longer care. Actually, I should have stopped caring a long time ago. When I open Lucy's message, I frown, because at first it appears to be a dark, grainy image. Then my eyes focus, and I see a mostly naked Lance asleep in her bed. And I know it's her bed, because I helped her pick out the spiral-print comforter that's covering him from the waist down. I frown, wondering why she'd send me the photo, and then a memory hits me—one of Lucy doing the same thing when she was dating a guy and found out he had a longtime girlfriend.

"Oh my God," I whisper, wondering how long they've been sleeping together.

"What happened?" My head flies up, and I shake it as Calvin comes toward me and takes my cell from my grasp. "Who is that?"

"Lance." He frowns at me, then looks back at the photo. "I should say, that's Lance in my friend Lucy's bed. I think that photo is her way of letting me know they're sleeping together." He eyes me warily, and I grin. "Isn't that great news?"

"Great news?" he asks, sounding confused. "I'm not sure it's great news that the people you considered friends back in Chicago are all assholes."

"I am." I take my cell from him and then hold down my finger on the image to save it. "This means whatever reason he had for doing what he's been doing is gone." I open the text from him and send the photo, along with a message that says simply, Leave me alone.

"Did you just send him that photo?"

"Yep." I look up and grin, then frown when I see the look on his face.

"Babe."

"What?"

His eyes roam my face; then he shakes his head. "Never mind. We'll deal with it when it happens."

"Deal with what?"

"Nothing," he says with a sigh. "Now, what do you want to eat? I'm gonna order our food."

"Kung pao shrimp and fried rice," I say. Then I ask, "What do you mean, 'deal with it when it happens'?"

"I don't have the energy to explain all that right now."

"Explain what?"

He leans into me, forcing me back until I'm lying on the bed and he's looming over me. "Give this to me, please," he pleads.

"What?" I breathe, knowing I'd give him pretty much anything as his weight settles over me and his eyes bore into mine.

"Right now . . ." He brushes his lips over mine. "I just want to order food, get into bed, and watch a movie with you," he says, his voice sounding rough and tired.

"Okay," I agree, and he runs his nose across mine, then kisses me softly. When he leans back, I'm a little disappointed to lose his warmth, but I hide it as I sit up and wipe my hands down the tops of my thighs. I watch him run his fingers through his hair, a move that seems somewhat agitated, and I bite my lip before asking, "Was everything okay on the phone?"

"Yeah, just my partner letting me know he didn't find anything new with our case and is heading home."

"I'm sorry."

"That's the way it goes sometimes." He pulls his phone from his pocket, then calls in an order for our food. When he's done, he tosses it on the bed, then reaches behind his head, catching me off guard as he takes off his shirt. He's not overly muscular, like he's spent too much time at the gym. He's sculpted like a piece of ancient warrior art. When he unbuttons his jeans, I hold my breath, and I must make a noise, because his eyes come to me and he grins as he kicks them off, leaving him in nothing but a pair of black boxers that are molded to his thighs and other parts.

"What movie do you want to watch?" he asks, going to the dresser and pulling out a pair of flannel pants he puts on quickly.

"Umm." I try to think of one movie out of the thousands I've seen, but it's difficult to think about anything with his chest and abs visible and just feet away.

"Anna, you with me?" He comes to stand in front of me, and I can't seem to peel my eyes off his torso.

"I can't think with you half-naked," I confess, and he laughs. "I'm not being funny, Calvin." I look up at him.

"Do you want me to put on a shirt?"

"I feel like that's a trick question." I eye his abs again, and he chuckles. "Maybe it would be for the best," I say with a sigh. "I don't think I can focus with you walking around like that."

"You're getting pink." He touches two fingers to my cheeks, then slides them down my neck to the edge of my T-shirt. "I'll put something on." He steps back, and I release the breath I was holding as he pulls out a shirt from his dresser and puts it on over his head. "Better?" He turns to face me.

"Not really, but it will have to do." I shift, feeling uncomfortable in my own skin, as if it's too tight and every nerve is waiting in anticipation for something to happen.

"How about I pick the first movie, and you pick the next one?" he suggests, going to the TV and reaching above it to grab the remote there.

"Sure." I get up off the bed and then ask, "What side do you sleep on?"

"The right," he answers, and I nod and walk around to the left side to get in, then rest against the headboard. He flips on the TV, pulls up a movie catalog, and clicks on *John Wick*. "Have you seen this?"

"No, is it good?"

"Do you like action movies?" he asks as he gets into bed next to me and wraps his arm around my shoulders, and I rest my head against his chest and my arm over his stomach.

"I like Keanu Reeves," I say, tipping my head back to grin at him, and he shakes his head and presses play.

Thirty minutes later, as I'm bawling like a complete baby because some bad guy killed a tiny adorable puppy, Calvin presses pause, then grasps my chin and turns me to look at him.

"Are you okay to watch this?"

"Are . . ." I sniffle. "Are any more puppies going to die?"

"No."

"Then I sh-should be okay." I pull my shirt up and wipe the tears off my face.

"Maybe we should watch something else."

"Is he going to kick their asses and make them pay?"

"Yes."

"Then I need to see that," I say, and he grins, then starts to lean in to kiss me but pulls back when the doorbell rings.

"That's dinner. I'll be right back." He quickly pecks my lips, then gets out of bed. A moment later, he comes into the room with a paper bag inside of a plastic one. "Do you want some wine?"

"You have wine?" I know I sound surprised.

"I got you a bottle on the way home."

"I think I love you," I say, then cover my face and groan. "I mean that in the friendliest way possible."

He laughs and walks to the bed, setting down the bag of food on the side table. "So I take it you'd like a glass of wine?"

"Yes, please. I'll help you." I start to get up, but he shakes his head. "I got it."

"Okay." When he leaves the room, I lean back, closing my eyes and tapping my head against the wooden headboard behind me. "'I think I love you.' Seriously, Anna?" I whisper to myself.

"Babe, do you want a plate?"

My eyes fly open, and I shake my head frantically as embarrassment creeps up my cheeks. "Nope, I'm good eating from the container."

"Be right back." He taps the doorjamb with his fist as he walks off, smiling. Even though I want to bang my head again, I don't, because with my luck, he'll catch me doing it. Instead, I fold my hands in my lap and mentally tell myself to stop being a dork and to act cool.

A few minutes later, he comes back carrying a beer, a glass of wine, and napkins. I take the glass when he holds it out to me and whisper, "Thank you." Once he's settled back on the bed, he opens the bag and hands me an overflowing container, then takes his out and starts up the movie.

We both dig into our food with abandon, and once I'm stuffed, I put the lid back on the container, then set it on the side table and lean back with my glass of wine. I take a sip, surprised when I find it's my favorite. I smile to myself and fight the urge to laugh at the craziness that is my life. A year ago, I never would have considered a movie date in bed with Chinese food and wine, or a date fishing on the lake, because those wouldn't have ever been options. Now I know what I was missing by dating men who would rather spend money on an expensive meal or a show that would bore me to death.

"Do you want another glass of wine?" Calvin asks as he presses pause on the movie, and I focus on him.

"I probably shouldn't. I need to drive home."

"I think you'll be sober enough to drive in the morning," he says, getting out of bed. "And don't think I'm letting you leave now that I've got you where I want you."

"In your bed?" I raise a brow.

"In my home." He picks up the bag and shoves the garbage into it, then grabs his container.

"In that case, I'll have another glass." I get up before he can tell me to stay put, and then I grab my container and follow him to the kitchen. He pours me another glass as I put our leftovers in the fridge. When we get back to the room, he shuts off the overhead light and closes the door, turning the room almost pitch black. I take a sip as he pulls back the covers, then set the glass on the side table as he lies down. I get in with him and lay my head on his chest as I watch him press play on the remote.

Not even two minutes later, I hear him snore softly, and I smile. I guess he wasn't lying when he said he was exhausted. When his hand on my hip tightens, I tip my head back and study his sleeping face for a moment, and then I curl myself deeper against his side. Before I know it, my eyes drift closed and I fall asleep, feeling safer and more content than I ever have in my life.

Suggestion 10

ACTIONS SPEAK LOUDER THAN WORDS

CALVIN

I wake when the bed shifts and instinctively reach out, grasping Anna's wrist before she can get away. "Where are you going?"

"The bathroom," she whispers.

I release her, roll the opposite direction, and sit up on the side of the bed as she goes into the bathroom. After flipping on my bedside lamp, I pick up the remote for the TV, turn it off, and then tap the screen of my cell to check the time. It's just after two, so I scrub my hands down my face, push up off the bed, and then open the door to the bathroom.

"Oh my God, I'm peeing here!" Anna squeaks from the toilet, and I look at her over my shoulder.

"I'm going to brush my teeth."

"Can you wait until I'm done in here?"

"I won't watch." I then turn around to face the mirror, grab my toothbrush from the holder, and load it with paste.

"Seriously?" she asks loudly.

I grin around the brush in my mouth, then turn on the water. "Better?"

"No, it's not better." The toilet flushes, and she walks to the second sink and flips it on to wash her hands. Once she's done, she stomps out of the bathroom and then comes back a second later with her bag over her shoulder.

"You're not leaving," I tell her, and she rolls her eyes at me in the mirror as she opens the bag and pulls out her own toothbrush. She starts brushing her teeth, and I decide not to ask her why she'd bring a toothbrush if she didn't plan on staying.

"Why are you smirking?"

"You're cute." I rinse my mouth, then shut off the water. "And even cuter when you're annoyed."

"I guess that's good, since you annoy me all the time."

"Do I?" I lean back against the counter, crossing my arms over my chest.

"It happens a lot." She rinses her mouth, then pulls out a package from the bag, takes a wipe out of it, and uses it to take off the little makeup she has on. Once she's done, she takes some kind of cream out and starts to rub it on her face.

"You sure did bring a lot of stuff to come over and watch a movie."

"Annoying." She glares at me out of the corner of her eye.

"What else do you have in there?" I reach over and try to peek in the bag, but she pulls it away before I can.

"Clothes for tomorrow," she says, still glaring, and I laugh. "I'm going back to bed." She brushes by me and heads back into the bedroom.

"That sounds like a great idea." I take off my shirt and start to kick off my pants.

"What are you doing?"

"Getting undressed." I look at her.

"Oh."

"Do you normally wear so much to bed?"

"No, not normally." She tugs at the end of her shirt.

"Feel free to get comfortable." I walk around to the opposite side of the bed from her.

She looks unsure for a moment, then strips off her pants and starts to lift her shirt, exposing her stomach and showing the lace of her panties, before dropping it back in place.

"Tease."

She laughs as I flip off the light, casting the room in darkness. I get into bed and reach across the distance between us, curling her into my side.

"Your bed is comfortable." She rests her hand over my stomach and her leg over my hip as my hand slides up her shirt to rest on the curve of her waist.

"It should be. I splurged on the mattress and will probably be paying for it for the next five years."

"How much did it cost?" She moves her head, and I know she's looking at me.

"A few grand."

"Really." She bounces her hip against the bed, causing her knee to rub up against my cock, which has been semihard since the moment we met.

"Babe."

"Yeah?" She tips her head back to look at me.

"I'm trying to be a gentleman."

"What?" she prompts. I take her hand and place it over my erection, and she whispers, "Oh."

"Yeah." I start to move it away, but she grips me tightly, and I groan. I find her mouth in the dark and sink my tongue between her lips. With my hand on her hip, I urge her to straddle me, and she whimpers as her lace-covered pussy rubs against my erection.

"Anna." I move my hands up her thighs, over her hips, and then to her sides. She leans back and pulls her shirt off, and I groan as I lift my head to pull one nipple into my mouth while cupping her other breast.

"Calvin," she hisses, sliding her fingers through my hair and tugging as she rolls her hips.

I release her breast and wrap my arm around her waist, holding her tight as I scoot back in the bed to rest against the headboard. "I want to see you." I reach over and flip on the light, and I look up at her beautiful face with her hair as wild as the look in her eyes. "Kiss me, Anna."

She drops her mouth to mine and grasps my shoulders as I hold on to her waist and slide my other hand into her hair, keeping her where I want her as I devour her mouth. I trail my lips down her neck, stopping to suck on her collarbone before moving to her breast. She fights my hold, wanting to rock her hips, but I know I'll lose it before I ever get inside her if I let her do that. "Calvin, please."

"Fuck, I like you calling out my name." I roll her to her back, causing her to gasp. "Let's see if I can make you scream it." I kiss her deep and hard before licking, nipping, and nibbling down her body, pushing her legs apart and holding her open. I let out a long breath against the lace covering her pussy, and she cries out. "You smell good." I press my nose against her, then slide my finger along the edge of the material, and her hips jerk.

"Please don't tease me."

"Why not?" I pull the material aside and roll my finger over her clit.

"Calvin."

"I like you like this, all needy and wet." I blow against her pussy as I fill her with two fingers.

Her back arches off the bed, and I pull her clit into my mouth and suck. I feel her start to convulse as she cries out my name once more and digs her feet into the bed, lifting her hips to meet my mouth.

"Yeah, I like that sound." I lift my face, lick and nip the skin on her belly, and then move up her body, giving the same treatment to both her nipples as her chest heaves. I lean back and lift both her legs, then remove her panties before dropping one hand to the bed and kissing up her neck. Her hands latch on to either side of my face, and she pulls my tongue into her mouth, making my cock throb.

"I want you," she breathes against my lips, sliding her hands down my back to the waistband of my boxers, and I help her remove them.

My cock aches as it nudges against her wet pussy, and I lose all rational thought as she wraps her legs around my hips and uses her strength to pull me forward. I slide into her, slowing myself and gritting my teeth. "I've never—fuck! Nothing has ever felt this good."

I pull out an inch and then slide back in two. With each thrust, she gets wetter and hotter, and the sounds she's making get louder, egging me on. Her tits bounce with each thrust, and her legs wrap tighter around my hips, trying to hold me hostage. I lean back and bend to pull one taut nipple into my mouth, then slide my thumb over her clit, rubbing in tight circles. She screams and her pussy contracts. The feel of her walls clamping around me makes me light headed, and I see stars right before I lose myself inside her.

"Are you okay?" I rest my forehead against hers as we both fight to breathe.

"I think so," she says with a sigh, and I laugh as I roll us so I'm on my back and she's half-sprawled over me.

I inhale deeply and run my fingers down her spine, still trying to breathe normally as her breath evens out against my chest. "Anna." I look down at her, then slide the hair off her forehead and see that her eyes are closed and her lips are slightly parted in sleep. I rest my head against the pillow and pull in a lungful of air.

I knew things between us were hot, but I had no idea just how hot until I got her under me. Who would have fucking thought that after years of searching and finding all the wrong women, I'd find the perfect one without even trying?

"So . . . you and the millionaire baker." Herb gives me a shit-eating grin as I walk toward my desk. "You never mentioned you were dating her, but apparently it's all over town that she was seen going into your house last night and didn't leave until this morning."

Fuck, my neighbors are nosy and have big mouths.

"We're seeing each other." I set down my coffee and take off my suit jacket before hanging it over the back of my chair.

"She's pretty."

"She is," I agree, even though it's an understatement.

"What's the deal with her ex? Rachel showed me the paper this morning after telling me the news about you two having a sleepover."

"They aren't together, and he's an idiot." I sit down. "And tell Rachel not to believe everything she reads."

"She didn't believe it. I guess she's gone into the bakery and met Anna a few times, and she knows you wouldn't date someone who was attached to someone else." He shrugs, and then we both look toward our captain's office when he shouts my name.

"Now what?" Herb asks.

"No idea." I get up and cross the open room.

"Close the door," Captain Sheppard commands as soon as I step into his office, and I shut it behind me.

"What's going on?" I cross my arms over my chest, unsure what to expect.

"Amy's parents have been cleared. I wanted to tell you personally." My jaw tics, and he holds up his hand, palm out. "I know you're pissed, but it's done, unless something else happens."

"Right." I nod, having no doubt they got off because of who they know and who they are in the community.

"Any updates on your two other cases?"

"Nothing to go on. We're going to follow up with a few people today and then go to where Mike's body was found. We'll walk the area to see if there are any homes with cameras facing the park or if there are any other eyes I missed in the area."

"Let me know what you find," he orders. I lift my chin, letting him know I heard him, and he sighs, knowing I'm pissed. "You can go."

I exit his office and take a seat at my desk. "What was that about?" Herb asks as he rolls his chair toward mine.

"He was just informing me that Amy's parents were cleared of any wrongdoing."

"Seriously?"

"Yep." I look over at him. "I guess it pays to be the son of the mayor."

"Asshole."

I don't agree verbally, even though I completely agree. "You ready to head out?"

"Yeah, but I'm in the mood for a cookie after Rach was going on about them all morning. You mind stopping at that bakery on Main so I can get one?"

"I thought you were watching your sugar."

"One won't hurt." He gets up and grabs his cell and a file folder off the desk as I pick up my coffee before heading for my truck.

When we reach the Sweet Spot, I open the door for Herb to enter before me; then I walk in behind him and spot Anna at the front counter. Her eyes come to mine, and the look that fills them makes me wish we were back in my bed.

"Hey, babe." I smile as I walk across the shop to the counter. "I want you to meet my partner, Herb."

"Hi." She turns to him and gives him a small smile as she holds out her hand for him to shake.

"You're prettier than the photo I saw of you in the paper," he tells her as he takes her hand. "And don't worry: my wife said you aren't uptight like the article made you seem." I catch Anna's smile faltering slightly. "She's met you before a few times. Her name's Rachel."

"I would probably know her if I saw her. I'm just not very good with remembering names."

"I get that," he replies, then drops his eyes to the display case. "She said you had some famous chocolate chip cookies."

"We do," Chrissie chimes in as she walks out of the back room. "They're over here on the end." She motions for him to follow her, and he heads that way.

I walk behind the counter to Anna, and she blushes as I take her hand. "Hey, baby."

"Hey," she says as I lean down to kiss her cheek.

"It seems better today," I tell her, referring to the shop, which is mostly empty except for a table taken up by two women drinking coffee, with what's left of a muffin between them, and a mom and her son sitting at a kiddie table. They're eating cookies—or the mom is eating a cookie while the little boy colors on the wall with chalk.

"I'm old news now." She shrugs, then looks to Chrissie. "I'm going to show Calvin something in the back."

"I'm sure you are." Chrissie winks and I chuckle.

As soon as we clear the doorway to the kitchen, I press her against the wall, out of sight of anyone who might see, and take her mouth in a deep kiss, then pull back and look at her. "I missed you."

"Me too." She leans back, and I focus on her face and can tell something is bothering her.

"What happened?"

"I got a message from my dad this morning. He and my mom are coming into town. They want to talk over dinner tomorrow. I was . . . I was wondering if you'd come with me."

"Of course." I cup her jaw, a little surprised she wants me with her. "Are you sure about having dinner with them?"

"No, but I'm hoping if I do, I can get them to finally listen to me. And if they don't . . . well, I guess that'll just prove it's time for me to move on and stop hoping they'll actually act like my parents."

"Did you hear back from your ex?" I ask, and she frowns like she forgot she had an ex.

"No, but I'm sure he got my message." I'm sure he did too; I'm also sure that when she sent him that photo, his first thought was that she was jealous, and then he made a list of excuses that could be believable as to why he was mostly naked in her friend's bed.

Not wanting to think about that asshole now, I change the subject. "What time is dinner tomorrow?"

"Probably late, around seven or a little after, since I don't get off until five thirty, six. I told my dad I'd make reservations somewhere. Do you know anywhere nice I can take them?"

"I'll make reservations this afternoon and let you know the details. I know of a few nice spots near the beach."

"Thank you." She leans into me and rests her forehead against my chin. "Knowing I'll have you there makes me dread dinner a little less."

"I'm here for you whenever you need me, Anna." I press my lips to the top of her head, and her arms wind around my waist. I hold her, sensing that's what she needs more than anything else.

"I should let you go. I know you're on duty."

"Sucks, but you're right," I say.

She pulls back and looks up at me. "Do you want to come to my place tonight?"

"How about you pack a bag and come to mine? I'm gonna go take my dog back today; it's easier to just let him out in the backyard than to try to chase him up and down the beach."

"That works for me. I probably won't be over till later, though. I want to check in on Edie. She came by yesterday before I went to your place, and I told her I'd see her tonight."

"That works. Just send me a message and let me know when you're on your way."

"Sure." She nods, and I kiss her once more before I pull her away from the wall.

Chrissie's eyes come to us as we walk hand in hand through the doorway to the front of the shop. "Well, that was fast," she says, smirking.

"I was going to say the same thing," Herb agrees as he takes a bite from the cookie in his hand, and I notice a box on the counter I'm sure is his.

I squeeze Anna's hand, and she looks up at me. "I'll see you tonight."

"Yeah," she agrees.

I drop a quick kiss to her lips, then look at Herb. "All right, old man, time to go."

"Fine." He picks up the box and calls out a goodbye to both women. When we get to my truck, I beep the lock, but he doesn't get in, instead stopping to look at me.

"What?"

"You really like her," he says, eyeing me like he's waiting for me to disagree.

"I told you we're seeing each other. It's not like I'd date someone I didn't like."

"You've got a point. Still, this is different. She's different." I know he's thinking about my ex, whom he never really liked. Vickie always made it clear that she wasn't happy with me being a cop, even saying that straight out around Herb and Rachel on more than one occasion. Herb's wife understood why Vickie was distressed, having been married to Herb for years. She knew the job sometimes pulled him away from his family, but she also knew that Herb's job was important to him and that she'd rather have him in her life than out of it. Looking back, I'm happy Vickie ended things before we got married or had a kid, which would have made the eventual end of our relationship even more complicated.

"I know," I agree. I walk around the hood and get in behind the wheel as he opens the passenger door.

"I'm happy for you, man. It's about damn time you found someone worth your time," he says as I start the engine, and all I can think is, *Don't I fucking know it.*

Suggestion 11

NEVER DRINK THE KOOL-AID

ANNA

"You cannot be serious," I hiss to the windshield as I pull into my driveway, half-tempted to keep going and run over the man who's standing next to a very annoyed-looking Edie. I shut down the engine and get out, taking my overnight bag with me, along with my purse.

"Anna." Lance hurries toward me with a worried look on his face, his tailored suit and perfectly styled hair seeming out of place in the laid-back town I've fallen in love with.

"Lance, I told you not to come, so I don't know why you're here."

"And I told him to leave, so I don't know why he's *still* here," Edie says, and I fight back laughter.

"I told you." He turns on Edie. "I need to talk to Anna. It's important."

"She doesn't want to talk to you," Edie huffs, and he glares at her the same way he used to glare at me whenever I said something that annoyed him.

"Edie's right, Lance," I say, and his gaze meets mine. "I don't want to see you. I don't want to talk to you, really. I don't want anything to do with you."

"If this is about Lucy, you need to remember you're the one who left me. I don't know what you expected me to do."

"Oh my God." I lean toward him and remind myself I'll be seeing Calvin later, and I don't want it to be because he's arresting me. "I don't care that you and Lucy are together."

"I'm not with her." His brows pull together as his mouth turns down at the edges.

"Okay, sleeping together." I roll my eyes.

"She doesn't mean anything to me. I love you."

"You don't love me, Lance."

"Yes, I do." He frowns. "Why else would I have asked you to marry me?"

"Because . . ." I shake my head. "I don't know, maybe money or my family or—"

"Money? Your family?" He laughs loudly, cutting me off. "Your family isn't as powerful as it used to be, Anna. My father told me before you and I started seeing each other that your dad's company is on the verge of bankruptcy."

"Your dad told you that?" I start to get a sinking feeling in the pit of my stomach. "Why would he tell you that?"

"Does it matter?"

"No, I guess it doesn't," I say, giving in, because this entire conversation is pointless. "It doesn't matter, because you and I are not together anymore."

"Anna—"

"Lance, I want you to hear me when I say what I'm going to say. I love it here. I'm happy here. I've made great friends, I have a job I love, and I'm seeing someone who's come to mean a lot to me. Please, just go home."

"You're seeing someone?" he whines, and my right cheek twitches as I drag in a breath in an attempt to get my temper under control. "I can't believe you're dating."

"Is that all you heard? Is that *really* the only thing you heard?"

"We were living together and planning our wedding."

"When we were together, how many times did you call me when you were away on business?"

"I don't know. I was working." He waves my question away like it's an annoying fly.

"How many times did we go out to have lunch when we were working in the same building?" I wait, and when he doesn't answer, I ask, "How many times did you stop by to see me, just because you missed me?"

"We lived together. I saw you every day. Why would I miss you?"

"That's my point, Lance." I lean toward him and point my finger at his chest. "For you, what we had was enough." I point at myself. "But it wasn't enough for me. I wanted more."

"More than my ring and my money?" There's a tinge of disgust in his tone. "Be honest, Anna. You got with me because I had money."

"No, Lance, that's where you're wrong. I got with you because I thought you were different. I thought I could love you and that you might be able to make me happy. I *stayed* with you because of your money."

He takes a step toward me, and my back straightens when his eyes narrow.

"Get off my property!" Edie says, getting between us with her hands up like she's ready to push him back if necessary.

"Go back to Chicago, Lance." I sigh tiredly as I pull Edie away from him.

"You wanna know why I was with you?" he asks, sounding disgusted, and I hold his stare. "Your daddy promised me half his company if I put a ring on your finger."

"Sorry you're not getting what you wanted."

"Oh no, Anna. I will, and when I get back to Chicago, I'm going to use every last resource I have to help my father buy the rest of your dad's crumbling company out from under him."

"I hope it makes you happy. Now if that's all, I'm going inside." I turn for the stairs to my place, taking Edie's hand and pulling her with me as I listen to Lance stomp off behind us. When we reach my apartment, I hear a door slam and tires squeal as he peels off.

"I can't believe you ever thought he was a nice man," Edie says when I let us both into my place.

"I know." I drop my bag to the floor. "I should've known he was like everyone else."

"Are you okay?"

"Yeah." I take a seat on the side of my bed and pull my hair back away from my face. "I know I shouldn't be surprised when the people from my old life show me their true colors. But I'm still surprised each time they do."

"It's because you wouldn't even think of harming them, even if it's just emotionally." She sits next to me and takes my hand. "Who is Lucy?" she asks, and I turn my head toward her.

"My friend."

"Why did he bring her up?" she asks, and I don't want to tell her the truth. I don't want her to know I've never made good decisions when it's come to friends.

"She sent me a photo of him half-naked in her bed, and I forwarded it to him, thinking that would be a good reason for him to leave me alone. I guess it was just a good excuse for him to show up here."

"Oh." Her nose scrunches in disgust. "I don't think you should consider her a friend."

I laugh loudly and fall back on my bed. "I don't. Really, I don't know why I ever did. She was never a very nice person."

She pats my leg. "Good thing you didn't drink the Kool-Aid in Chicago. Seems to me it's poisonous."

"It seems that way," I agree as her eyes lock on mine.

"How was your night with Calvin?"

"Perfect." I can't help my smile.

"I bet." She winks, and I groan. "Oh, stop. I might be old, but I'm not dead. I want to know everything."

"We're never talking about anything that happens between Calvin and me."

"You're no fun."

"Sorry." I sit up. "I love you, but I just can't talk to you about that stuff."

"Fine," she grumbles. Then she asks, "When are you seeing him again?"

"Tonight." I get up, grab my bag from the floor, and place it on the bed. "I just need to repack."

"So you're sleeping over at his house again?"

"Yeah." I meet her gaze. "Unless you wanted to do something?"

Her eyes fill with mischief. "I've been meaning to clean out the downstairs storage closet. You could help me with that."

"Very funny." I smile, then tip my head to the side and ask, "What are you doing tomorrow?"

"Me and the girls are taking a painting class in the afternoon, but after that, I don't have any plans."

"Do you want to have dinner with me, Calvin, and my parents tomorrow night?"

"Your parents?" Her brows rise as her eyes fill with surprise.

"They want to talk to me. We're having dinner around seven. Calvin's going to make reservations for us." She stands as I ramble, then gently takes my face in her hands. "You don't have to come," I tell her softly as I look into her eyes.

"I'm coming." She plants a kiss on my forehead, then lets me go. "I want to be there when you ask your dad about offering that jerk part of his company to marry you."

I'm not looking forward to that conversation. "Thank you, Edie." Over the last few months, Edie has become the mother I always wished

I had growing up, and I can't imagine dealing with my parents without having her there to offer support.

"You're welcome. Now finish packing and go see your guy." She walks to the door, then looks at me over her shoulder. "I would tell you to not do anything I wouldn't do, but I would do it all, so I don't see the point." With that parting statement, she leaves, and I throw my head back and laugh. Once I have my hilarity under control, I finish packing and call Calvin to let him know I'm on my way.

"Bane, I missed you," I say with a laugh once I've arrived. He jumps up on the fence with both paws to greet me, and I rub his head as he tries to get close enough to lick my face.

"It's safe to say he missed you too," Calvin says, and I smile over at him. "Hey, babe."

"Hey." My chest warms in a way that's becoming familiar, and he smiles as he shakes his head before leaning over the fence to kiss me. I pull back, laughing and wiping Bane's slobbery kiss from the side of my face.

"Bane, down!" he orders with a chuckle, and Bane falls from the fence as Calvin opens the gate and takes my bag off my shoulder.

"Did you make any headway in solving your cases today?" I ask as he takes my hand to walk the short distance to the front door, making me wonder if I will ever get used to the way I feel when I'm around him. I hope I don't. I hope I always feel this flutter of excitement in the pit of my stomach when I'm in his presence.

"No." I hear a hint of frustration in his tone, frustration I know isn't directed at me. We talked a little this morning about what he's working on—not details, just that he's trying to solve the two murders that happened recently, and so far he's hit nothing but dead ends.

"I'm sorry."

"It happens." He gives my hand a squeeze before letting it go to pull open the door, and once he's closed and locked it, he carries my bag toward his bedroom and says over his shoulder, "I picked up the stuff to make spaghetti, or we can order in if you're in the mood for something else."

"Spaghetti sounds good to me." I stop when Bane blocks me from going any farther; then I laugh as he pivots and shoves his head under my hand so I'll pet him.

"He'll get used to having you here." I lift my eyes off Bane to meet Calvin's gaze. "Until that happens, he's going to be all over you for attention."

"I don't mind." I rub behind his ears one last time, then step around him. I take my purse off my shoulder when my cell phone rings and then pull out my phone, shaking my head when I see it's Lucy calling. I don't press ignore like I want to. Instead, I swipe to answer and put it to my ear. "Yes."

"I've been trying to get ahold of Lance," she says bitingly. "He's not answering. Is he with you?"

"No."

"Oh." She lets out a breath. "I thought—"

"You thought he'd show up here and I'd fall into bed with him," I say, cutting her off. "I'm not you, Lucy."

"I know you're upset, but you never appreciated him the way I do. I love him, Anna."

"And I hope you're happy together, but for the love of God, both of you just leave me alone." I hang up, switch my phone to silent, and shove it in my bag.

"I'm gonna go out on a limb and guess you forgot to tell me something?" Calvin says, and I focus on him. When I see his expression, I realize I should have told him about Lance being in town.

Crap.

"Um . . . Lance was outside with Edie when I got home from work tonight."

"You didn't think to tell me about this earlier?"

"It wasn't a big deal." His eyes narrow, and I press my lips together, knowing that was the wrong thing to say.

"What did he want?"

"We didn't really get into what he wanted. I told him to leave. He thought I was upset about him and Lucy, but I told him I wasn't, then told him to leave again. We argued a little more, and then I found out my dad offered him half of his company if he asked me to marry him."

"Jesus."

"He might have mentioned plans to destroy my dad's company." He stares. "Oh, and I need you to add Edie to the reservation for dinner. She's coming with us tomorrow."

"I'm not sure it's a good idea for me to come to dinner, Anna. The way I'm feeling right now, I might just kill your father."

"I'm not very happy with him either right now." That's an understatement.

"I'm also pissed at you for not calling me when you got to your place and Lance was there."

"It was fine." I wave off his concern. "Edie was there. It wasn't a big deal."

"I can see you love Edie, but she couldn't have helped if he'd tried to hurt you."

"He wouldn't do that."

"I bet you never thought he'd sleep with your friend either." Damn, he has a point. "People are unpredictable. He's proven he's willing to go to extreme lengths to get your attention. So please, if something like that happens again, call me."

"Should you being all protective make me tingly?" I ask, trying to ease the tension I feel coming off him, but he doesn't even crack a smile. "Fine," I agree with a sigh. "I'll call you."

"Good, now come here so I can kiss you properly," he orders.

I close the distance between us, and as he wraps his arms around me, I rest my hands against his chest. "Sorry for not telling you about

Lance showing up. Honestly, once he was out of sight, I'd forgotten about his existence until Lucy called."

"I don't want to talk about him anymore tonight." He gives me a squeeze.

"Okay, what do you want to talk about?"

"You can tell me exactly where I make you tingle." His hands glide down my back to my bottom as I lift up on my tiptoes to get my mouth closer to his.

"Or I could show you." I smile and nip his bottom lip.

"I like that idea," he growls. He lifts me off the ground and carries me to his bed, where he has his way with me.

An hour and two orgasms later, I walk into the kitchen wearing Calvin's T-shirt and my panties and watch him come out of the pantry with a jar of red sauce, along with a box of pasta, in nothing but a pair of plain black sweats.

"What can I do to help?" I ask as he stops to kiss me on his way to the counter.

"You can grab the meat from the fridge." I run my fingers along his abs as I walk away, then open the fridge and frown when I see a bouquet of pale-orange roses on the shelf inside.

"Those are for you." Arms wrap around my waist, and he presses a kiss to my neck as I pull the flowers out and hold them to my nose, which is stinging.

"Why?" I turn to meet his gaze.

"I thought of you when I saw them." He kisses my neck, then reaches around me to grab the ground beef off the shelf.

"So they aren't apology roses or 'it's your birthday' roses; they're just because you were thinking of me?"

"Yeah."

"Thank you." I fight back stupid girly tears.

"I don't have a vase, but I'm sure there's something in one of these cabinets you could use." He motions around the room.

"Do you mind if I look?" I ask, inhaling the scent of roses once more.

"Make yourself at home, baby," he says, and I open and close cabinets until I find a red oversize plastic cup with a handle and lid, the refillable kind you get from the gas station.

"Is this okay to use?" He nods, and I fill it with water, then cut down the stem of each flower carefully before arranging them in the cup. When I'm done, I place them on the counter and admire them for a minute before I go to where Calvin is now browning the meat in a pan, slide my arms around his waist, and kiss his shoulder. "Thank you for the roses. I love them."

His hand covers mine on his stomach, and he tips his head down toward me. "You're welcome." I slide under his arm and rest against him, then hear him sigh when his phone rings on the counter next to the sink.

"Take it. I'll finish with this." I take the spatula from him, and he kisses the side of my head.

"I'll be quick."

"Don't rush," I murmur as he picks up his phone, walks out of the kitchen, and puts it to his ear. I finish browning the meat, then pick up the jar of sauce and try to open the lid, banging it against the counter in frustration when it won't budge.

"I'm so sorry, baby." I turn as Calvin comes toward me, now dressed in jeans and a long-sleeved flannel shirt with his badge clipped to his belt, carrying his shoes. "I have to leave."

"Is everything okay?"

"There was a big accident. They're asking everyone to come in to help clear it. I shouldn't be gone long." He takes a seat on one of the chairs and puts on his shoes. I set down the jar and walk across the room to him, and he runs his hand up the back of my bare thigh.

"I'll finish dinner. We'll eat when you get back."

"Thank you." He stands and kisses me swiftly, then looks down at Bane, who's waiting to find out what's happening. "Take care of Anna," he orders, and then, before I can blink again, he's gone.

I look down at Bane when I hear the front door close, and he falls to his stomach and rests his head against his paws with a groan.

I go back to the counter and pick up the jar of sauce, groaning to myself when I can't get it open no matter what I try. I chew the inside of my cheek, then go to the pantry to see what he has and come out with an array of beans, one onion, a can of chopped tomatoes, and tomato paste. I place the already cooked meat in a bowl, then chop up an onion and add it, the tomatoes, some of the tomato paste, and a few spices to the pan. I cook it all down before adding the beans along with the meat. I taste it when I'm done and smile. It's not spaghetti, but it's delicious. I just hope Calvin likes chili. I set it to simmer and clean up the kitchen; then, with nothing to do, I go to the living room and search for the TV remote. When I don't find it, I take a seat on the couch, and Bane joins me in the quiet, and we both end up dozing off.

I blink my eyes open when Bane starts barking and then sit up and push my hair out of my face. "Bane, come here," I call, and he runs into the room, barks at me, and runs back out as the doorbell rings. I push off the couch and go to the front door to look out the etched glass, seeing what looks like a young woman on the porch.

My insides twist with unfamiliar jealousy. Calvin and I just started seeing each other, and I'm sure a man who's as attractive as him dated a lot. He could still be dating now, since we haven't discussed if we're exclusive, which is something dumb to think about now, especially since we've had sex multiple times. I open the door and see it's not a woman but a girl who looks about fifteen or sixteen.

"Anna?" She smiles as I hold on to the door to keep Bane inside.

"Yes."

"I'm Sam, Herb's daughter. Calvin called my mom. He said he's been trying to get ahold of you, but you weren't answering. He asked her to send me over to check on you."

"Crap, my phone is on silent. Please, come in." I rush to the bedroom and pull on a pair of sweats from my bag, then get my phone out of my purse. When I turn on the screen, I see I have over ten missed calls, three voice mails, and a few texts. I step back into the hall and see Sam getting down on the floor with Bane, who obviously knows her well. "I'm just going to call him back really quick."

"Sure." She smiles at me as Bane rests fully on her lap.

I dial his number and put my phone to my ear.

"I've been trying to get ahold of you," he says as a greeting.

"I'm so sorry. I fell asleep on the couch, and my phone was on silent. Is everything okay?"

"Besides worrying about you? Yeah, everything's fine. We're finishing up now. The fire department just left, so I should be home within an hour or so."

"You shouldn't have been worrying about me. I'm okay," I tell him as I walk down the hall toward the kitchen to check on dinner.

"Babe, your ex is in town. You've had nothing but drama since I met you. I'm not taking any chances."

"It hasn't been all drama," I lie; it's been complete drama since we met.

"Anna," he says with a sigh.

"Anyway. I'm fine, and I'll see you when you get home."

"See you when I get home, and tell Sam I said thank you for coming to check on you, even though I'm sure she was happy to have a reason to drive, since she just got her license."

I laugh, remembering the sense of freedom I felt when I first got my license. "I'll tell her."

"Later, baby."

"Bye." I hang up and walk back down the hallway, and Bane takes his attention off Sam and comes to me. "I'm so sorry you had to come over," I say, rubbing the top of his head as she gets up off the ground.

"It's cool." She smiles, then tips her head to the side. "So you and Calvin are dating?"

"Yeah." I can't help the smile that tips up my lips.

"Awesome, that means I'll see you again, since he's around all the time," she says, and then her phone rings and she pulls it out of her pocket, groaning and tipping her head back to the ceiling before putting it to her ear. "Hey, Mom. Yes, she's here. She was asleep and her phone was on silent. I know . . . I know . . . yes, Mom, I know . . ." She groans once more. "I'll be home soon . . . Mom, I'm not an idiot. I know not to pick up hitchhikers. Bye, Mom." She hangs up and looks at me, and the giggle I've been trying to control escapes, and she laughs along with me. "My mom is crazy."

"She loves you."

"I know, but seriously, she's crazy. Like, where the heck am I even going to see a hitchhiker in town?"

"You can never be too safe."

"I guess," she mutters, then looks at Bane. "Do you think Calvin would notice if I took him home with me?"

"Probably." I smile as Bane goes to her like he knows what she's said.

"Sorry, big guy, you gotta stay here." She rubs the top of his head, then looks at me. "It was cool meeting you, Anna. I'm sure I'll see you around."

"I hope so," I say, meaning it.

She turns for the door, opens it, and calls over her shoulder, "Later, Anna."

"Get home safe, Sam, and please don't pick up any hitchhikers!"

Her laughter fills the house as she leaves, and Bane whines at the door while pawing it. "Sorry, buddy. You're stuck with me for now," I tell him, and then I go back to the kitchen. "Do you need to go outside?" I ask, and he starts jumping around like he's a tiny puppy instead of a huge dog.

I open the back door and step outside with him, wrapping my arms around my waist as I watch him run around before stopping in the middle of the yard and lifting his leg. When he's done, he comes back to me, and I start to head back up the steps to the house, but he takes off again. "Bane, come on. Time to go in," I say, and he runs back with a ball in his mouth, then drops it at my feet. "Oh, you want to play." I pick up the yellow tennis ball and toss it in the air one time, and he woofs. "Sit," I order, and he does. "Stay." He watches my hand, and then, as soon as I bring my arm back to throw it, he springs to his feet. I let it go and watch him take off and then catch it as it bounces across the yard. He brings it back to me and drops it again, so I pick it back up and lose myself in the simple act of playing fetch.

"You made chili?"

I jump and spin around to face Calvin, and Bane barks as he runs across the yard to greet him.

"I couldn't get the jar of spaghetti sauce open," I admit, and he smiles as he comes down the steps toward me. "Seriously, they must have glued it on. I even tried the banging-against-the-counter trick, but it didn't work."

"I should have opened it before I left." His arms wrap around me, and I snuggle into his embrace.

"It's okay. I just hope you like chili."

"I hate it," he says.

I look up at him and search his eyes. "You're joking, right?"

"No." He laughs. "My mom used to make it all the time when I was a kid. I hated it. I'm pretty sure the shit you found in the pantry was left over from the last time she took it upon herself to go shopping for me."

I giggle and rest my forehead on his chest. "I'm sorry. I didn't know."

"I'll make myself a sandwich."

His fingers curl around the back of my neck, and I soak in the feeling of being in his arms, of being safe and content. I searched for the feeling of contentment for years, but it wasn't until I gave up everything I thought was important that I actually found it. I wrap my arms around him, wishing I could express exactly what he's coming to mean to me.

"Let's eat and get to bed. I'm sure you're tired after the day you had."

"Besides Lance showing up, it's been a great day." I tip my head back toward him. "Thank you."

"Anna," he whispers, looking into my eyes as his fingers sweep my jaw.

"It's odd, because we haven't known each other very long, but I want you to know I like this; I like being with you. I like the way you make me feel. I like that you show me you care without using words." I lean up and touch my lips to his. "I like you."

"Baby, you gotta know I feel the same," he says gently against my lips, and I smile.

"I'm glad your mom made you come apologize." I laugh when he groans.

"Are you ever going to let me live that down?"

"Nope," I say as he lets me go and opens the door. "Where would be the fun in that?" I ask, and he smacks my bottom, making me squeal in laughter. I turn on him, and when I see the look in his eyes and he starts to advance on me, I hold up my hands. "What are you doing?"

"Nothing." He takes a step toward me, and I take a step back. "What's wrong, Anna?"

"Why are you looking at me like that?"

"Like what?"

"I don't know, like you're the Big Bad Wolf and I'm one of the innocent little pigs you want to eat."

"That sounds accurate. I do want to eat you." His eyes roam over me from my hair to my toes.

My breath hitches, the space between my legs tingles, and my nipples pebble. "Calvin."

"I'm right here, Anna."

"I thought . . . I thought you were hungry."

"I am." He steps toward me again, but I'm too lost in the look in his eyes to retreat. "I'm always hungry for you, Anna. Since the moment we met, you've created a hunger in me that's insatiable. No matter how many times I've had you, I want more. I can't get enough of you."

I lean into him when he cups my jaw. My eyes slide closed, and I pray I never lose this.

Suggestion 12

MAKE YOUR OWN PATH

ANNA

I come awake when warm breath puffs against my face, and I open my eyes to see Bane's snout, right before he greets me with a wet doggy kiss.

"Bane." I roll to my back laughing and wipe my cheek as he puts both his paws on the bed to rest his head against my stomach. I sit up and rub behind his ears, then look to the door when Calvin appears wearing black jeans with an open button-down shirt and holding a cup of coffee.

"I was coming to wake you, but it looks like he beat me to it." His gaze roams my face and hair, and his expression warms with contentment, a look I like seeing from him.

"He did. I even got a kiss." I pull the blanket up and tuck it under my arms as he comes toward me, holding out the cup of coffee. I take it from him, and he puts one knee on the bed and captures me behind the neck, angling my head before dropping his mouth to mine. "I like your good-morning kiss more." I open my eyes and get lost in his.

"I hope so." He smiles as he runs his fingers along my cheek before they fall to his hip.

I take a sip of coffee, then glance at the clock. "You're up early."

"I have to leave in thirty minutes. I'm taking Bane to training, then have an early meeting."

"Oh." I start to push back the covers. "I'll get ready and leave when you do."

He shakes his head and places his hand on my thigh to keep me where I am. "Stay. I'll give you a key. You can just lock up when you go. And tonight when you get off work, just use it to let yourself in."

"You're not going to be here?" Dread at the idea of not having him with me tonight fills my chest, and I drop my eyes from his to my lap.

"I haven't forgotten tonight is dinner with your parents, Anna." His hand captures mine, and I lift my head when he squeezes my fingers. "I wouldn't forget something as important as that. I'll be home in time to take you."

"Sorry. I should have known you wouldn't forget. I . . . it's just going to take me some time to trust this isn't too good to be true, that *you* aren't too good to be true."

"I'm not perfect, baby, not by a long shot. And I don't want you to think I am. Perfect is an impossible standard to live by."

"You're not like any man I've known." I cover his lips with my finger when he starts to open his mouth to say something. "And I know you aren't perfect, but in the short time we've known each other, you've taken more care with me than anyone I have ever known, and I appreciate that."

"Fuck, I'm gonna be late."

"What?" I ask.

And he suddenly takes the cup of coffee from me and places it on the side table before he uses his weight to push me back on the bed, which means I'm laughing when he kisses me.

~

I step out of the bakery and lock the door. After grabbing my cell out of my bag, I look at the screen and see a text from Edie asking if I can pick her up, along with giving me her location. I text her back, letting her know I'm on my way, and then head for my car, parked in the lot down the block. When I pull up in front of the painting place, I see Edie, Pearl, and Dixie outside on the sidewalk, laughing as they look at their paintings, which look like they're mostly of naked men. I roll down the passenger window and shout, "Edie!" I get her attention, and she waves wildly.

"Anna, my beautiful, sweet girl," Edie says loudly when she opens the door to my car and falls in with her canvas as Dixie and Pearl open the back door and attempt to get in at the same time.

I look among the three of them and shake my head. "Are you guys drunk?"

"A little," Edie says as she fumbles with her seat belt and the two in the back seat finally get in and seated.

"I thought you were at a painting class?"

"We were," Dixie replies, shoving her painting between the front seats so I can see it and narrowly missing hitting me in the face with it. "We had a live model today. Isn't he handsome?"

I study the painting and press my lips together. The model might have been handsome, but his offset eyes, awkward smile, and overly square jaw make him look like something you'd see in a nightmare.

"It smells like you ladies drank a case of wine."

"We had three bottles of wine, not a case," Pearl corrects me. Then she adds, "That's just one bottle each."

"Thank you for setting me straight," I murmur as I pull out into traffic. "So where is everyone going?"

"To Edie's. We heard you're having dinner with your parents tonight, so we're going to help you two get ready," Pearl says.

I inwardly groan. "I'm going to Calvin's to get ready."

"Call him and tell him that he can pick you up at Edie's. He won't mind," Pearl says.

She's right; he won't, but still. "I really don't need help getting ready."

"We know you don't, but it will be fun!" Dixie sings.

"Fine," I say, giving in.

"Can you make one quick stop first?" Pearl asks.

"Sure, where?" I meet her gaze in the rearview mirror.

"The liquor store."

"I think the three of you have had enough alcohol today."

"It's not for us. It's for you."

"Okay then, I don't need a drink."

"Sure you do," Pearl insists.

"I don't," I deny with a shake of my head.

"You do."

"I don't. I might need a glass of wine when it's over, but not before. Trust me: I need to have my wits about me when dealing with my parents."

"Oh, I guess that makes sense," she agrees, and I sigh. "But I still want to stop. I need to buy a lotto ticket. I'm feeling lucky."

"You say that every week, and every week, you waste your money," Dixie tells her.

"One day, I'm going to hit it big, and when it happens, you'll be singing a different tune."

"If you hit the lotto, I'll eat my words and run through the streets naked."

"Now I really need to stop," Pearl says with a laugh, and I can't help but smile.

"I wouldn't mind a slushy. The gas station on the corner near the house has them," Edie tells me, and I wonder if this is how a mom feels when dealing with small children. I bet it is.

"Fine, but you guys have to be fast," I say as I pull into the gas station.

"I'll make sure they're quick," Dixie tells me as she pats my arm before getting out with them. I watch them go into the store, and ten minutes later, I watch them come out with their hands full of junk food and drinks, looking like teens who had free rein in a convenience store.

"Now, are you ladies ready to go home, or would you like me to make a stop at Chuck E. Cheese's so you can see how many tickets you can collect?" I ask as I back out of my parking space.

"We're too old for Chuck E. Cheese, but feel free to stop at Dave and Buster's," Pearl quips, and both Edie and Dixie laugh.

"You three are trouble."

"We've been told that a time or two," Edie says. Then she adds, "But when you reach our age, you earn the right to live life on your own terms."

"That we can agree on," I say as I pull in and park next to Edie's car, which has had a tarp over it ever since her license was suspended.

"I miss your car," Dixie sighs from the back seat.

"I need to sell it," Edie murmurs as she unhooks her belt.

"Pardon?" I ask as Dixie and Pearl get out, slamming the doors.

"My car—I need to sell it. Will you help me take some pictures and post it online?"

I turn toward her in my seat and reach over to take her hand. "There's still a chance you can get your license back."

"I know . . . ," she agrees, looking away. "But my eyesight isn't what it used to be, and my reflexes have slowed. I shouldn't be driving, and I'm smart enough to know when to cut my losses."

"Edie," I say softly, hating the defeat in her tone.

"I'm not upset." She turns to face me once more.

I study her to see if she's being truthful, and when I see she is, I squeeze her hand. "In that case, I'll help you with whatever you need."

"Thank you." She lets me go and pats my thigh. "Now, call Calvin, and I'll see you inside."

"I'll be just a minute."

"Take your time." She gets out and shuts the door, and I grab my cell phone from my bag and call Calvin. When he doesn't answer, I leave him a voice mail, then send him a text in case he doesn't check his messages. I get out and head inside Edie's house without knocking, and then I spend the next hour with three women who have shown me in a short time that life is all about doing what makes your soul happy.

"That would be Calvin!" Edie shouts from her bedroom as the doorbell rings, and I get up from the sofa, smoothing out the skirt of my black halter-top dress, and make my way to the front door in my heels, which are already killing me.

As soon as I open it, I wonder if it would be wrong to call off tonight, because all I really want to do is make Calvin take me back to his place, where I can properly express how gorgeous he looks in his all-black suit.

I start to open my mouth to tell him he looks handsome but snap my mouth shut when his hand slides around my waist and pulls me against him. He drops his mouth to my ear. "I can't believe I have to share you with your parents and Edie when you look like you do right now."

"I was thinking the same thing," I breathe, and he leans back to catch my eye and smiles.

"Though I want your hair down. I prefer it wild." He touches his lips to mine, and I automatically touch my hair, which I pulled back into a chignon.

"Oh my goodness," Pearl says, making me jump, and I look over my shoulder at her. "You two look so good together. Don't move. I need to get a picture for your mom."

"Christ, it's like prom all over again," Calvin mutters, and I laugh as she spins around and heads back down the hall, probably to get her cell phone.

"You went to prom?" I ask him, and he looks down at me.

"Yeah, didn't you?"

"No, I didn't get asked, so I pretended like I was too cool to go," I tell him truthfully.

"You didn't get asked to prom?" he asks, but before I can answer, Pearl comes back with her phone pointed at us.

"Maybe you should come in and stand in front of the fireplace."

"Pearl," I say with a sigh.

"Fine, where you are will work. Smile." I lean into Calvin and place one hand on his chest as he curls me deeper into his side, and the flash on the phone comes on, almost blinding me. "This is perfect." Pearl walks away and looks at her phone as Edie comes around the corner.

"I'm ready."

"You look stunning, Edie." Her two-piece cream-colored pantsuit reminds me of something my mom would wear, only Edie wears it better, because she has a navy-blue tank tucked into her pants instead of a stuffy blouse and a bold sapphire necklace that's obviously costume jewelry but still extraordinary.

"You two look gorgeous together." She smiles at us, and I smile back, then focus on Pearl and Dixie when they come down the hall carrying their bags.

"Do you guys need a ride?" I ask, knowing neither of them drove here.

"We're going with you to the restaurant," Dixie informs us with a smile.

My brows pull together. "What?"

"No, you're not," Calvin states.

"We won't sit with you until Anna's parents take off. When that happens, we'll all have dinner together."

"We're having dinner with my parents." I tell them something they already know.

"You're meeting with your parents. I'll be shocked if you have a meal with them, especially with Edie and Calvin there with you," Pearl says.

"What does that mean?"

"It means the people in your life who care about you won't accept your parents' hurting you. So when they try—which my guess is won't be long after you sit down—either Calvin or Edie will say something they won't like, and they'll take off."

Damn, she might have a point. Neither Calvin nor Edie will sit by and let my parents say anything that might hurt me.

"You're still not coming to dinner," Calvin says, and I look up to see him narrowing his eyes on Dixie and Pearl.

"You're going to a public restaurant. We happen to be going to the same one. You won't even see us unless Anna's parents leave."

"Did you know about this?" Calvin asks Edie, who has a slight smile forming on her lips.

"I had no idea, but I have to say I like this plan."

"We don't really have time to argue about this," I cut in. "We're supposed to be at the restaurant in ten minutes, and it's at least fifteen minutes away."

"Fine. Everyone, load up in my truck. But just so you ladies know, I will have no issues arresting any of you if you piss me off."

"I need wine," Edie says, ignoring Calvin's statement and walking past us, with Pearl and Dixie agreeing with her as they head for his truck. He beeps the doors unlocked.

"How did you become friends with the Golden Girls?" he asks when I turn to follow them.

"I don't know how it happened; it just kind of did." I shrug.

His eyes lock on mine. "You do know the three of them are trouble, right?"

"Yep." I step outside with him and lock Edie's front door. "I still love them."

"That's because you're just as crazy as they are."

"Maybe," I agree as he walks me to the passenger door, opens it, and then helps me in.

Once he's behind the wheel, he takes my hand and places it on his lap, and I start to bounce my knee, feeling anxious for the first time today.

"It's going to be okay," he says, and I turn to look at him as he covers my hand and laces his fingers through mine.

"I know," I say quietly. "I just hope it isn't a huge mistake meeting with them, and it's not helping that I don't know what they want."

"You promised them dinner, and when dinner is over and they go back to their hotel or back to Chicago, you don't owe them anything else."

"You're right," I agree, and he lifts his chin ever so slightly. Then we drive the rest of the way to the restaurant in silence, my mind playing all the ways in which tonight could go wrong.

"Unbelievable." My father sits, flashing his napkin in the air before resting it over his lap. "We haven't seen you in months, and you bring strangers with you to dinner."

"Like I told you, they aren't strangers. Calvin and I are dating, and Edie is my friend." I bite out each word clearly, when what I really want to do is scream and storm off. Since the moment I introduced Calvin and Edie to my parents outside the restaurant, my father has been uglier than he normally is, which is saying something, and my mom has acted like she has no clue what's going on.

"You must admit, darling, that it was very rude not to let us know you'd be bringing guests," Mom says with a frown as she picks up her fork and examines it.

"You know what I think is rude?" Edie asks, picking up her glass of wine and taking a sip. "I think you two are rude."

"Who are you, besides my daughter's 'friend'?" Dad uses air quotes on the word *friend*. "You're rather old."

"She's not old, and I live in her house," I say in her defense, and Edie pats my leg.

"So you give her money." Dad rolls his eyes. "Figures."

"You did not just say that," I hiss, and Calvin covers my hand as I start to get up from the table. "Apologize to Edie."

"Do not tell your father what to do, young lady," Mom says, finally looking at me.

"I'm not a child, Mother. I can do what I damn well please."

My father stands suddenly and leans over the table toward me, placing his finger close to my face.

My eyes widen, and then suddenly I'm moved back and Calvin is standing in front of me, blocking my view, and his voice is rumbling through the room. "Do not ever get in her space again."

"Do not tell me what to do, and get your hand off me," Dad grunts.

I try to peek around Calvin, but I can't see anything from my position.

"Sit down now or I'll take you down to the station and book you for the fuck of it."

"I forgot you're a police officer. It would be interesting to see what might happen if I make a couple phone calls while I'm here in town."

"You don't scare me." Calvin moves slightly, and my dad makes a sound while my mom whimpers. "But you should be scared."

"Do you know how many people are witnessing you accost me?" Dad asks, sounding like he's slightly in pain.

"You're not in Chicago. These aren't your people. They're mine," Calvin informs him. "Your name might hold some weight there, but you don't have any control here."

"I can't believe you're spending time with a man like him, Anna," my mom whispers, sounding horrified, and I'm sure if I could see her face, it would look twisted.

"And I can't believe you two are her parents," Edie says, then looks at me. "Maybe you were switched at birth. I think you should have a DNA test done."

"You gave up your life to spend time with people like these?" Dad asks, sounding disgusted.

I stand and bump into someone, but I don't look to see who it is behind me. "If you mean caring, considerate, loyal, and accepting, then yeah, Dad, I did. Though I didn't have much of a life to give up, and I honestly wouldn't trade what I have now for any amount of money, because you can't put a price on happiness."

"I'll give you five million to come home."

I snort. "Did you not hear me? There is no amount of money you could give me that would make me change my mind."

"Tell her."

I spin, knowing the voice behind me, and when I see Lance, anger makes my stomach clench.

"Why are you here?" I hiss, glaring at him.

"You think I didn't love you, Anna, but you should know I did," Lance says, looking devastated, and my stomach twists for a different reason.

"Lance."

"I lied. I was pissed and hurt. What I said about the reasons I asked you to marry me wasn't true, but I was mad enough to make a few phone calls after I left, and I found out—"

"Shut up!" Dad shouts, cutting him off, and I turn to see his face is red.

Calvin puts his hand in Dad's face, then turns to Lance. "Say what you need to say."

"Who are you?" Lance asks Calvin.

"Young man, now isn't the time for a pissing contest. If you have something to say, then say it," Edie says with a sigh.

"Is everything okay here?"

I look over at Gaston, and I notice Tyler is with him as well, along with Chrissie and Leah, standing slightly behind their men.

My cheeks warm with embarrassment, and I wonder if we could become any more of a spectacle. Then I know the answer when Pearl and Dixie join everyone else standing around the table.

"This is ridiculous." My dad tosses his napkin on the table, then looks at my mom. "We're leaving."

"You own seventy percent of the shares in the McAlister Corp. Your grandfather put them in your name when you were born, because he didn't trust your father not to sell off the company," Lance says.

"What?" My question is barely audible.

"That's why he told me he'd give me half the company when we got married. There was a clause that stated if you were married, your husband, then eventually your children, would be given equal shares of the company. That's why he and my father got together and hatched a plan to get us together."

"Jesus," Calvin growls.

I swallow as I look at my father. "I never wanted anything to do with your company. I would have signed it all back over to you if you'd asked me to."

"That's because you're an idiot." His nostrils flare. "You don't understand the value of money."

"No." I shake my head. "I understand the value of money. I just know money doesn't make you happy."

"That's where you're wrong."

My heart sinks. "I feel sorry for you. For both of you." I look between him and my mom. "I hate that you believe that." I look at Lance. "Thank you for being honest with me."

"Can we talk?" he asks. He tucks his hands in his pockets, looking as nervous as he did the first time he asked me out.

"No," Calvin says before I can answer, and I hear women, young and old, burst out laughing.

I want to smile, but I hold it back and shake my head. "I don't think we have anything to talk about, but I really do wish you nothing but the best."

"I had the best, Anna, and for what it's worth, I'm sorry I didn't look into this. I should have looked into why he made me that offer."

"It doesn't matter. It's done," I say, and he nods, glances at my parents with disgust clearly written on his face, and then walks away.

"We're leaving," my father says as he helps my mom out of her chair.

"My lawyer will be in contact," I tell his retreating back, but he doesn't stop to respond. He and my mom both leave without giving me a second glance.

"God, I thought they'd never leave," Pearl says, and then she looks at Gaston, Tyler, Chrissie, and Leah. "Do you want to join us for dinner and drinks?"

Chrissie and Leah look at each other, then at me.

"Please, join us," I tell them.

"I'm going to talk to the manager and have him get someone to rearrange the tables for us," Gaston says, then kisses Chrissie's cheek.

"I don't know if it'll be that easy, Gus," Chrissie tells him, looking around the packed restaurant.

"I know the owner," he says, then looks at me. "Happiness isn't based on money. It's based on who you know." He winks and I laugh.

"You okay, baby?" Calvin asks, blocking everyone out and wrapping his arms around my waist.

I look up into his eyes and drop my forehead to his chest. "I don't know what that means. I don't know how I feel about what just happened," I admit quietly, and his hand rubs my back.

"I get that."

"Thank you for being here," I say, and he slides his hand up the back of my neck and uses his fingers to tip my head back.

"There is nowhere else I'd want to be but right here with you."

"Even with what happened and everyone joining us for dinner?"

"Even with that," he says quietly, dipping his head to brush his lips against mine.

"Aren't they so darn cute?" I hear Pearl say, and I look around Calvin's back just as the flash on her phone goes off. "Oh, I love that one!" she cries as I blink away stars.

"Let me see," Chrissie says, holding out her hand to see the photo. Then she squeals, "It's perfect!"

"Do you think they'd notice if we took off?" Calvin asks, and I tip my head back to him, grinning. His eyes roam my face; then he sighs and turns, holding on to the back of my chair until I'm seated and then helping me scoot in before he takes his own seat.

"Are you okay?" Edie asks, and I focus on her.

"Yeah," I reply, and she studies me for a moment, then pats my hand and picks up her wineglass.

A minute later, Gaston comes back to the table with two waitresses and a man who looks like he owns the place, and he asks if we can follow him. He leads us to a back room that's mostly empty, and before we even take our seats, the waitstaff take our drink orders, then come back with baskets filled with warm bread and fresh butter.

When our drinks arrive, Edie taps her fork against an empty glass, cutting into everyone's conversations. "I'd like to make a toast." She picks up her glass filled with wine, and everyone follows suit. "To unexpected love, unexpected friendships, and unexpected good times with good people." She looks around. "Cheers."

"Cheers," I whisper, feeling Calvin's hand holding mine tightly as I look around the table, filled with people who have come to mean a lot to me. What I told my father is true: I wouldn't trade all the money in the world for what I have. I know what it's like to have money. I know what it's like to be able to afford anything my heart desires. But I know more than most that money won't feed your soul like love and true friendships will. And if I'm honest with myself, I hate that my parents have never experienced true happiness before, that they will never know the difference between those who are around because they think you can give them something, and those who are around because they truly care for you. I guess I'm lucky in a way, because now I appreciate what I have a little more.

Suggestion 13

Don't Let Your Ego Get in the Way

CALVIN

I let myself into Anna's place with the key she gave me two weeks ago and take off my jacket before laying it on the end of the bed. I turn toward the fridge and stop to watch Anna through the glass of her balcony door, a blanket wrapped around her shoulders, a glass of wine in her hand, the moon and stars casting a glow around her. From her stillness, I know she's lost in thought, and I'm sure it has something to do with her phone call to her lawyer today.

It's been a month since we had dinner with her parents: a month of her coming to terms with her father's deceit and a month of her trying to figure out what to do with the shares she owns in a company she's adamant she doesn't want. I'd like to say I'm okay with her having millions of dollars, but the truth is, it makes me uncomfortable. Not because she has more money than I could ever make in my lifetime but because it's a tie to her old life that I don't want her to have.

Sighing, I grab a beer from the fridge, open it, and then head outside.

"Hey." She tips her head back to greet me, and I bend to kiss her before rubbing the top of Bane's head and taking a seat in the chair next to hers.

"How was work?" she asks as I take a pull from my beer.

"Good, busy." I take her hand and kiss her fingers.

"Did you get the break you've been waiting for?"

"No." Her expression softens, easing the frustration I feel. My two murder cases have gone cold, which is to be expected when you don't have a suspect, a witness, or a motive.

"I'm sorry."

"Me too," I say with a sigh. I take another pull from my beer before asking, "What did your lawyer say?"

"Nothing new. I just need to decide what I'm doing."

"You have time to figure that out."

"I know. It's just I'm torn. Part of me wants to keep everything out of spite, but another part of me wants to sign it all over to my dad and wash my hands of the whole thing."

"You'd give it all back to him?"

"Most of it." She shrugs. "I'd keep a few shares to give our kids, but I have no desire to have so much control over a company."

Fuck, I like the idea of her having my kids, but I know the first time I asked her if she wanted children, she seemed unsure. "Our kids?"

She looks at me and rubs her lips together. "I . . . I didn't mean to imply that we're going to have kids. I just—"

"I want two," I say, cutting her off before she can take it back and piss me off. "A boy and a girl, but if we have two boys first, I want to keep trying for a girl."

"You know, people who say that always end up having either nothing but girls or a bunch of boys."

"I'm good with a bunch of boys."

"Okay." She rolls her eyes. "But what if you get all girls?"

"I guess I'll figure out how to deal if that happens."

"Right," she says with a laugh and then sighs, resting her temple against the back of her chair. "You're lucky I love you, Detective Miller, because you make me crazy."

"Or maybe you're lucky I love you," I say, and her pupils dilate. And I know then that she didn't even realize she said she loved me and hadn't expected me to feel the same. "I'd like to remind you that I have to deal with your crazy friends and family and whatever drama you cook up."

Her eyes search mine before she whispers, "I don't cook up drama."

"Okay, you don't, but you're a magnet for it."

"That seems to be true," she agrees.

I chuckle, then lift her hand to my lips. "I love you, Anna, everything about you, even the things that make me wonder if you might be certifiable."

Her lips tip into a smile. "I'm going to ignore everything you said."

"Everything?" I ask, and she sets down her mostly empty wineglass and gets up, only to sit sideways in my lap.

"Not all of it." She rests her hand against my cheek, then touches her lips to mine. "I'll remember you said you love me. I like that part." I smile and slide my hand up her back to thread my fingers through her hair.

"Are you tired?"

"Why?"

"Just curious." I enjoy the feel of her in my arms, her smell washing over me, and the look in her eyes that says she's just as content as I am in what we are building.

"Then no."

"Good, neither of us have work tomorrow, which means I don't have to rush things tonight." I stand with her in my arms, and she wraps her arms around my shoulders.

"You've rushed things before?" She raises a brow as I open the door and step inside.

"If you haven't noticed, I'm not going to tell you," I say, and she laughs and then gasps as I lay her on the bed and spend the rest of the night taking my time, showing her just how much I love her.

I jerk awake when Bane barks and paws at the curtains covering the glass sliding door, and I sit up, tossing back the covers.

"What's going on?" Anna asks as she sits up.

"I don't know. Stay here." I stand and grab my jeans from the floor. I put them on before walking the few steps to the door. After opening the heavy dark curtains, I look out at the bright morning. "Heel," I order Bane, and he falls to his stomach, whining. I open the door and step outside, leaving him inside with Anna, and look around. When I don't see anyone nearby, I start to head back in but stop when I smell weed. I look over the rail of the balcony and close my eyes, saying loudly, "I'm going to pretend you three are not smoking weed right now!"

I listen to the three women on the deck below let out surprised screams. They stumble and fumble before the door to downstairs opens and closes. I go back into Anna's and rub Bane's head to let him know he did good, since he's been in training to sniff out drugs, and that's the first time he's been alerted outside of a training situation.

"What happened?" Anna asks, and I notice that at some point she's put on a shirt. I go to the kitchen to get a cup of water and flip on the coffeepot.

"The Golden Girls were outside getting high. Bane must have smelled it," I say. I then go to the bathroom, take care of business, and brush my teeth before shutting off the light. I then find Anna just where I left her with a wide-eyed look on her face.

"They were getting high again?" she asks, and I narrow my eyes on her. "I—"

"I don't want to know." I hold up my hand, palm out. "I'm going to pretend it didn't happen, because the idea of dragging the three of them down to the station and dealing with them on my day off is too much for me to think about right now."

"I don't think they do it often," she says, chewing the inside of her cheek.

"Baby, I don't care if people smoke weed, but it's not legal in South Carolina, which makes it a crime. And since I'm a cop, I'm on the side of the law when it comes to dealing with it."

"I get that. I'll talk to them," she offers, and I shake my head.

"You are not talking to them about it. They are all grown—very grown—women who know they shouldn't be smoking pot. They don't need you to tell them that."

"I actually think they might have a whole *Freaky Friday* thing going on, like they switched consciousness with three sixteen-year-old girls. Only unlike that movie, they don't want to change back, because now they have an excuse to do whatever they want, and that excuse is they're old."

I laugh at her explanation, then mutter, "You might be right. Maybe I should search for three teen girls who spend their time knitting, baking cookies, and taking care of a bunch of cats."

"If you find them, I can contact a witch; then you can lock the six of them in a cell together, and we'll force them to return to their bodies," she says with a laugh, and I grin.

"Where are you gonna find a witch?"

"Online." She shrugs. "You can find anything with the help of Google."

"True." I pour her a cup of coffee and add creamer and sugar, and then I pour myself a cup and take both to the bed. I hand hers over, then sit with my back to the headboard.

"I need a TV," she says, sitting back and then taking a sip from her mug.

"You don't."

"Yeah, I do. I know you like to watch the news in the mornings. I should get one for when you're here."

"Anna, we love each other, and last night we spoke about having kids one day. I don't know about you, but I'm thinking that means it's time for us to talk about you moving in with me."

"You want me to move in with you?"

"Yeah." I frown. "You do realize we haven't spent a night apart since the first night we spent together, and more often than not, you're at my place. Plus, I like this place, but it's not exactly where I see us living or raising a family. I can span the space in three steps."

"Okay," she says, taking another sip of coffee. "I'll talk to Edie later today and see how much time she needs before I can break my lease without hurting her pocket."

"That was surprisingly easy," I mumble to myself, and she laughs.

"Do you want me to argue with you about it to make you feel better?"

"No, just talk to Edie and let me know what she says. Then we'll get you completely moved in—not that you seem to have much." I look around.

"None of this is mine. Well, besides the clothes in the closet, stuff in the bathroom, and the bedding."

"You said you had a place in Chicago. You didn't have house shit?"

"No, I did. I still have my stuff in storage there. But I'll probably just let it go if I'm going to move in with you."

"Why wouldn't you keep it?"

"Well, none of it would exactly fit in with the theme you have going on at your house, and none of it holds any real sentimental value. Plus I have no real desire to go back to Chicago to get it all and then drive it back here."

"If we live together, it will be our house. I want you to be comfortable there and add your touch."

"I can do that." She grins, with happiness filling her eyes.

"And I can see about getting a week off in the fall, and we can fly out to Chicago and drive your stuff back here," I say, and I notice her expression dull immediately. "You really don't want to go back to Chicago."

"My life is here. My friends and the people who've become like family to me are here. Chicago is my past, and I don't want to go back. I just want to keep going forward."

"Don't give up your storage unit. You might feel differently about going back there in a month or a year," I tell her, and she studies me for a long moment before she nods. "All right, now . . . our plans for the day."

"I didn't know we had plans today." She smiles as she takes a sip of coffee.

"Our plans involve a meeting with the kitchen designer, Amanda, who's coming to my place at one. I need to sort that out before you officially move in. Otherwise, my mom will lose her shit."

"I can't imagine your mom losing her . . . you know."

I grin. Over the last few months, I've learned Anna doesn't cuss, which is adorable. Especially when I know she wants to. I've also noticed she never says anything when I cuss.

"She was on me about me fixing up my place before we got together. Now, anytime I talk to her, the first question she asks is when I'm going to make the house somewhere you might want to live."

"I love your house." I notice a hint of worry in her voice.

"I know, baby."

"And you know it doesn't matter to me how the kitchen looks or anything else, right?"

"I know why you're with me, Anna. I've never second-guessed why I want to be with you or why you want to be with me."

"Okay," she says quietly, chewing the inside of her cheek—a tell that lets me know she's not convinced, unlike the twitch she gets in her cheek when she's getting angry or frustrated.

"I don't have money, Anna, not much anyway, and the life we build, I want us to build it together. What's mine is yours and vice versa."

"I don't want the stocks. I don't want any of it, not even a few shares for any kids we might have. I don't want any ties to the reason my parents are the way they are."

"I don't give a fuck what you do with it, Anna. Keep it, sell it—it doesn't matter to me."

I see the tension leave her shoulders and the worry leave her eyes. "Thank you." I lean over and kiss her and then back away when there's a knock on the door and Bane barks. "That's probably Edie," she says. Then she shouts toward the door, "Just a second!"

"Anna, is Calvin with you?" Herb's voice rings loud, surprising me.

I see her frown as I call out, "I'm here, Herb."

"Christ, man, I've been trying to get ahold of you!" he shouts back through the door, and I get up off the bed, searching the side table for my cell that isn't there.

"Just a sec." I wait for Anna to pull on a pair of pants, and once she's got them on, I go to the door and open it.

He steps forward, looking wired. "Hey, Anna, you good?" he asks.

"Yeah, Herb, you?"

"Been better, sweetheart," he says, then looks at me. "I've been calling you for the last hour."

"I must have left my cell in the truck last night. What's going on?"

"We have another murder." I glance at Anna and catch her wringing her hands together.

Fuck.

"Let's talk outside," I say, then look at Anna. "I'll be right back, baby." After I get her nod, I step outside and shut the door behind myself. "Where?"

"One of the hotels. The body's been there a couple days. Housekeeping didn't go in before today, because the 'do not disturb' sign was left on the door."

"Fuck."

"It's bad." He jerks his hand through the hair on his head, looking away. "The scene looks like something out of a horror movie. He was killed in the shower. It looks like he didn't know it was coming and was stabbed multiple times in the back before he was able to try to defend himself, which was pointless, judging by the defensive wounds on his hands and chest."

"Let me get dressed, make sure Anna's okay, and then I'll meet you. Send me the address," I say and then shake my head, remembering I don't know where my cell is, and if it's not in my truck, I'll be driving around to every hotel in town. "Never mind. What hotel is it?"

He rattles off the hotel and room; then, with not much of a goodbye, he disappears down the stairs. I pull in a breath, then turn and open the door.

"You have to go," Anna says as soon as I step inside.

"Yeah, baby, I gotta go." I grab my shirt off the end of the bed and shrug into it, then pick up my shoes and take a seat to put them on. "I don't know how long I'll be, but it'd help me out if you met with the designer for the kitchen. It took a couple weeks to get that appointment. If you can't, I can ask Mom."

"I'll go," she says as she walks to the kitchen, where she pours a cup of coffee into a travel mug. "I'll explain you had to work and see if they can reschedule." She brings me the cup, and I take it as I stand.

"You know what I want to do, baby, and if you have ideas, give it to them. Just let them know so they can start getting quotes on the job."

She looks a little unsure, but still she says, "Okay."

"Thanks." I plant a quick kiss on her lips, then head toward the door, stopping with my hand on the knob to look at Bane.

"He's good. I can take him with me."

"If you find my cell around here, call Mom. She's got Herb's number. If it's in my truck, where I think it is, I'll call you when I can."

"I'll see you at home," she says simply, and it's that constant easy acceptance of my job that proves why she's not just right for me but perfect for me in every way.

"I'll see you at home." I kiss her once more and then leave, forcing myself not to think about her, the life we're building, or anything else that doesn't have to do with the man whose life was taken sometime within the last couple of days.

I park in the lot of the hotel and get out of my truck before sending Anna a text to let her know I've got my cell so she doesn't go searching for it. I walk past the two cruisers parked outside along with the crime scene van and enter the lobby, not stopping to talk with the uniformed officers talking near the front desk. I go to the elevator, and once it opens, I get in and press the button for the fifth floor. I follow the signs to the room and spot Herb outside on the phone, near the door. When he sees me, he ends the call and comes toward me.

"Fill me in," I say, and he turns to walk at my side.

"Victim is Paul Bieben, forty-two, married with three kids, in town on business. His wife spoke to him two days ago when his flight landed, and he told her that he was going to check into his hotel and rest but would call her before he went to bed."

"Did he call?"

"No, she said she sent him a couple messages but didn't hear back from him. She said that wasn't unusual, but when he didn't call the next day, she started to get worried and tried calling him. He didn't answer, so she tried the hotel and was told no one under that name was staying there."

"Is this the hotel he told her he was staying at?"

"No, and the room isn't under his name. It was booked under the name Andy Storm."

"Was he having an affair?"

"His wife said they've had issues with infidelity in the past. That's why she stopped looking for him when she called the hotel and found out he wasn't there, and she decided to pack up her kids and drive from Georgia to Florida, where her sister lives."

"Do you believe her?" I ask, knowing jealousy can make people act out of character.

"Yeah," he says as we stop outside the open door to the hotel room, and he hands me a pair of shoe covers and gloves.

"Are you ready?"

"We're never ready," I admit as we walk into the room and past the bathroom, where I see police photographer Jim Jenkins taking photos. "Let me know when you're done," I call into the bathroom, not wanting to get in his way but still seeing spots of blood on the walls, along with red smeared around the sink and on the floor.

"You got it, Calvin." He lifts his chin.

I walk farther into the room and stop in the middle to look around. The first thing I notice is that it's clean, with a suitcase unzipped but closed on a stand between the dresser and TV stand, with pants and a shirt lying neatly on top. On the side table next to the bed, there's a phone, the room's key card, and an open book placed facedown on the wooden surface, like the person reading it had set it there knowing they would be back. The bed is unmade, the top cover falling off the end, the sheets wrinkled and in disarray, with the pillows in the same state of mess. Besides the bed, nothing in the room looks out of order, which isn't exactly unusual, but having stayed at hotels a few times, I know the longer you stay, the more you relax. Eventually, you stop closing your suitcase and leave a few pieces of clothing around the room, or even a glass or two.

"It doesn't seem like he was in here long."

"It doesn't," Herb agrees.

I walk to the bedside table and study the items there, the book quickly catching my attention. The title, the couple on the cover intertwined in an embrace, and the blurb all surprise me. "This is a romance?"

"Yeah, I noticed that."

"Not many men read romance novels." I pick it up carefully and can see the wear on the corners of the pages, like it's been read a few times. "Get me an evidence bag for this," I say, and he calls out for one, and an officer appears a moment later holding a few. I bag the book and hand it to Herb. "We need to get that dusted for prints. If it belongs to whoever did this and their prints are on file, we might have a suspect."

"I've also got a couple guys going over the video for the hotel. They have four cameras. One in the elevator, two in the lobby, and one on the parking lot. When you see the amount of blood in the bathroom, you'll agree with me that whoever did this wouldn't have been able to leave without carrying some evidence out with them when they left."

"Cal, I'm done," Jim says as he comes into the room. "I'll let the rest of the team know to give you a few minutes before going in to finish up."

"Thanks, Jim," I tell him, and he lifts his chin before leaving.

I walk back down the hall with Herb and take two steps into the bathroom, where the stench of death has permeated the air. I study the wounds on the man in the shower, then look at the blood-soaked towels on the floor next to him, the splatter on the tiled walls and ceiling.

"Where's the murder weapon?"

"I have guys searching the trash for the weapon, but so far we've got nothing, so either they tossed it or took it with them," he says, then nods toward the sink. "It looks to me like after they knew he was dead, they attempted to clean up."

"It was too much for them." I notice a streak of what looks like dried puke on the toilet seat, along with what appears to be smeared blood on the rim. "They might've wanted to clean up, but they couldn't follow through. Someone should've seen something, and there should be evidence on video. There's no way the person who did this left without being noticed." I lock eyes with him. "Have you spoken with management?"

"There are three managers at this hotel: one night, one day, and one who picks up shifts for the two of them when they have time off. The guy who picks up is here today. From the records, we know the night manager was on when Paul checked in, and we're waiting for him to come in."

"Do we know if there was anyone staying in the rooms on either side of this one?"

"There was a couple next door. I spoke with them earlier, and neither of them heard or saw anything," he says, and I follow him out to the hall and slip off the covers on my shoes and my gloves, dropping them in the trash bin next to the door.

"Cal, Herb, we got something on video," Steve, one of the uniformed officers, says as he comes down the hall toward us.

"We're coming," Herb calls back, and Steve turns around as we follow him to the elevator and get in to head down to the lobby.

"What do we got?" I ask, studying the grainy image on the TV monitor in the manager's office.

"The picture is shit, but it's obviously a woman getting on the elevator a little after midnight, and we see her again, walking through the lobby and out to the parking lot. We lose her then, but a silver Mustang is visible in one clip a few minutes later."

"Please tell me we got a plate number?"

"No plate, but watch this," he says, pressing play on the video, and it shows the inside of the empty elevator. The door opens, and a woman steps on and looks directly at the camera in the corner.

"You've got to be shitting me," I hiss, staring at the black-and-white image of Sandy Burton, the same woman who came to speak with me after Chris Davis's murder.

"Doesn't Sandy drive a silver Mustang?" Herb asks, and I look over my shoulder at him. "And I'll have to check with Rachel, but I'm pretty sure she set up a book club, because she's big into romance novels."

I look back at the screen and shake my head, finding it hard to believe that she would have it in her to commit murder, especially after seeing the violence involved in Paul's death. "We need to bring her in for questioning."

"Let's hit the road and track her down. I know she works out of her house. If we're lucky, she'll be there," Herb says. He pulls his phone out of his pocket and leaves the room.

"Steve, can you email me those clips?"

"Yeah, man, I'll send them now."

"Thanks." I pat his shoulder.

I meet Herb at his SUV and get in on the passenger side. "Rachel confirmed that Sandy drives a Mustang and is a huge fan of romance books. She even said she carries a paperback with her wherever she goes, which she said is weird, because everyone else she knows uses e-readers, unless they're going to the beach or something."

"Do you think she did this?"

"I don't know, but she was there," he says as he backs out and drives through the hotel lot toward the exit.

"She was, but what did she use as a weapon? We know Paul was stabbed multiple times, and the murder weapon wasn't left at the scene. I don't know of any object that's normally left in a hotel room for a guest that could be used as a weapon, which means if she did this, she had to have had it on her."

"Do you think she planned it?"

"I'm not sure." I run my fingers through my hair, my mind spinning.

"Are you thinking what I am about her coming in and asking about what happened to Chris?"

"That she was fishing to see if we had any leads?"

"Yeah," he says as he turns onto the highway that leads to the area in town where Sandy lives.

"If she killed Paul and Chris, what would her motive be?"

"I don't know. I guess that's a question only she could answer. Do you know who Paul was having an affair with?"

"His wife said it was someone from their town. That said, he traveled a lot for work, so who knows if he had multiple affairs that she didn't know about."

"Idiot."

"Yeah," he agrees with a shake of his head.

We drive the rest of the way in silence. I'm sure, like me, he's trying to fit the puzzle pieces together, even the ones that don't fit so easily. When we pull up in front of Sandy's house, the first thing I notice is her Mustang in the driveway, the same year and model from the surveillance video.

"How do you want to play this?" I ask as we park.

"This is just routine questioning. She was seen on video, and we want her to come in to find out if she knows anything."

"Got it." I check my weapon before I hop out and then meet Herb at the hood. When we reach the front porch, I open the screen door and lift my hand to knock, but a chill slides down my spine when I see the door is slightly ajar. I look at Herb and he shrugs.

"Sandy?" I shout into the house, and when I get no answer after calling her name three times, I draw my gun. I push the door open and step into the entryway.

"I'm calling this in," Herb says, and I lift my chin.

"Sandy?" I raise my weapon and walk farther into the house, through a mostly dark living room where trophies, awards, and crowns are placed on shelves lining each wall, a clean kitchen, and then a hall lined with closed doors. The first one I clear is a bathroom, the second what looks like an office, and the third a small bedroom.

I close my eyes when I reach the last door in the hall and call out Sandy's name; then I place my hand on the knob, turn, and push the door open. I scan the room. I see a folded piece of paper on one of the bed pillows, jewelry placed neatly on the dresser, and a pile of clothes on the floor in the corner of the room, with blood on them. I head into the bathroom and find it empty. Herb then enters behind me.

"She left a note," I tell him.

"It's addressed to you." He hands it over, and I open it, hoping it'll give us some kind of insight into where she is and why she did what she did.

Suggestion 14

FIGHT WITH EVERYTHING YOU HAVE

ANNA

I park in Calvin's driveway and look at the house before searching deep within myself for even the smallest bit of doubt about moving in with Calvin. Not surprisingly, there is none. All I feel is contentment and excitement about starting a life with him. The only real worry I had was washed away after Calvin left this morning and I spoke to Edie about moving out. I was a little nervous about her reaction, but I shouldn't have been. She told me she was happy for us and that I shouldn't waste a second thinking about my apartment, since she gets inquiries about it all the time and isn't worried about it staying vacant for long. She did make me promise that I would come over for wine a few times a week, a promise I look forward to keeping.

"Well." I look over at Bane, who has his head hanging outside the car. "Are you ready to go in?" In response, he pulls his head inside, and I roll up the window and shut down the engine. I get out and pat my thigh so he'll get out with me, and he sticks to my side as I grab my overnight bag from the trunk and head through the gate and up to the front door. After I let us both inside, I drop my stuff in the bedroom, then go to the kitchen and start a pot of coffee. Calvin told me that he won't be home until late, and I know he's going to want to relax when he gets in, and hopefully I can help him do that by making him a nice meal. I pull up my shopping app and start a list, figuring I'll go to the grocery store when the designer leaves. I glance at the clock and see I have about thirty minutes before the appointment with the kitchen designer, so I fix myself a piece of toast and then take it, along with a cup of coffee, out the back door, letting Bane out as I go. I sit on the step and look around the yard. I'm excited about the idea of putting my touch on it and the house. With a table, some chairs, and a few lights, this will be the perfect space for us to entertain outdoors in the summer when we have our friends and his family over, and when we have kids, there will still be plenty of space left over for a small swing set and slide—maybe even a cool tree house.

Just then the doorbell rings, and I force Bane to stay outside so he doesn't trample the designer with love. I put my coffee cup on the counter, then head down the hall and look out the glass pane on the side of the door at a woman standing on the porch. Even though her image is somewhat distorted by the etched glass, I can still make out her large mass of hair and her full face of makeup.

"Hi." I smile as I open the door, then hold out my hand, trying to place the familiar-looking woman as she steps into the house. "I'm Anna. Calvin said to tell you he's sorry he couldn't be here. He had something come up with work, but I can show you around the kitchen and walk you through our plans for the space."

"Oh." She looks slightly surprised. "That would be great."

"Great," I say with a smile. "The kitchen's just down the hall." I turn, listening to her heels clicking on the hardwood as she follows me.

"So you and Calvin are together?"

I smile at her over my shoulder. "Yeah."

"It must be serious if he's trusting you with the task of helping design his kitchen."

"Do you know Calvin?" I ask, trying not to get annoyed by her nosy comment, especially since she's here to do a job.

"We went to school together," she says as I stop near the sink. "I've known him for years." Calvin never mentioned that the designer was a friend when he told me about the appointment this morning. "Do you live here?" she asks, looking around.

"I'm moving in." I rinse out my coffee cup and feel her move behind me.

"Why you?"

"Sorry?" I turn to face her and notice she's much closer than before.

"I just don't get it." The anger in her tone and the odd glint in her eyes put me on alert. "He was so closed off after his ex left him; then you two cross paths, and all of a sudden he's throwing himself at your feet?"

"I don't know why he chose me," I tell her softly, hoping to calm her as Bane starts to bark at the back door, pawing it to get inside.

She shakes her head, taking her eyes off me to look around. "I don't get it either. I tried to get his attention, but he barely even spared me a glance whenever we were in the same place." She turns back to me. "It's not supposed to be like that, you know. Everyone knows that when you see the person meant for you . . ." She pauses, looking at me expectantly. I'm not sure what she expects from me, so I simply nod. "You know it; you just know it. I knew he was supposed to be mine the first time we met. I just needed to wait until he noticed me." She runs her fingers along the edge of the counter. "He didn't; he never did."

"I'm sorry . . ." God, why didn't I ask her name when I let her into the house?

"Sandy," she says, and I take a step back from her when she moves closer. That is not the name of the designer Calvin told me.

"I'm sorry, Sandy, but maybe you should come back when Calvin is home and talk to him about this."

"It's too late." She starts to pace back and forth as pink spreads up her cheeks. "It's too late to tell him how I feel. I've already done too much. I-I-I didn't mean to . . . I just wanted his attention and thought that if he had a reason to spend time with me, he'd finally feel what I feel. He will never love me now. He won't love me now, but that's okay. It's okay—we have the next lifetime to get it right." She locks eyes with me. "That's how it works, you know."

"How what works?" I ask, my voice shaking as I spot my phone on the counter across the kitchen and move closer to it as Bane's barking gets louder.

"Soul mates—you meet them in each lifetime, over and over and over and over. You just have to be able to recognize them. He didn't recognize me this time, but next time I'll make sure he does . . . I'll make sure."

Oh God, she's crazy.

"Sandy, I think . . ." I lick my lips nervously. "I think you should leave and come back when Calvin is home and explain all this to him."

"He'll be here," she says, taking her purse off her shoulder and pulling something out of it before dropping her bag to the floor. "He's a good cop. He'll figure out it was me and go to my house and see my note. He'll be here." She glares at the back door. "I can't think with that barking."

"What are you doing?" I rush toward her when she walks toward the back door, but then she turns and lifts her arm, and that's when I see the gun. It's so small that it almost looks fake, but I know it's not. It's the same type of gun Lucy used to carry in her purse.

"Don't come any closer," she demands, and every inch of me freezes in fear.

"Okay. It's okay." I hold my hands up in front of me. "I won't move, I promise. I won't move, but don't open that door. Bane is just a puppy, and he's excited that someone is here and wants to come in to say hello. He doesn't know any better." My voice hitches as tears clog my throat.

"Tell him to shut up." She raises the gun higher and aims at the center of my chest.

I close my eyes as a tear tracks down my cheek; then I pray that Bane listens. "Bane!" I shout as loud as I can, and he stops barking at the sound of my voice. "Quiet, and place," I order, and he must be obeying because the barking doesn't start back up. I take a breath and remind myself that she's right about one thing: Calvin is a good cop, so he'll be here soon.

"Calvin is my soul mate," she says suddenly, and I open my eyes and watch her rip her hand through her hair.

"I know," I whisper in agreement when I see her finger press down on the trigger ever so slightly.

"I don't want to do this, but I need to be with him. I should be with him, not you." Her hand starts to shake, and my heart pounds. "I don't like hurting people."

"You don't have to hurt anyone." My voice is barely above a whisper as I stare down the barrel of the gun pointed at me. "Calvin wouldn't want you to hurt anyone. He'd never want you to hurt anyone."

"I know." Her chin wobbles; then her eyes and the hand holding the gun fly to the side when the doorbell rings. "Who is that?"

"I . . . I don't know." I swipe away the tears on my cheeks as I attempt to breathe.

"Get rid of them," she hisses, and I whimper in fear when she swings the gun back in my direction. "Now."

I jump and hold up my hands. "Okay . . . just please don't point that at me," I beg, and she lowers it to her side, then glares at me when the doorbell rings once more, and Bane starts to bark again.

I walk down the hall with my heart pounding, feeling her right behind me, then stop when she presses the gun into my lower back and places her mouth close to my ear. "Do not be stupid." I nod, unable to speak, then let out the breath I'm holding when she takes a step back.

With my hand shaking I open the door and attempt to smile at the woman in a navy-blue pantsuit with a briefcase in her hand whose eyes latch onto mine. "Ca . . . can I help you?"

"I'm Amanda from Custom Designs, and I have a meeting scheduled with . . ." She glances at the iPad in her hands. "Calvin Miller."

"He's not home."

"Oh." Her brows knit together. "Do you know when he'll be back?" *Hopefully soon*, I think but don't say as I shake my head in a negative motion, and she looks at me like I might be crazy. "Just let him know that he needs to reschedule with the office."

"I'll let him know."

"Thanks." She turns to walk away, and I wait until she's far enough away that she should be safe before I shove all my weight into the door behind me. Sandy grunts as it rams into her. Knowing this is my only chance to get away, I take off on a run across the porch and down the steps, then scream as the sound of a gun firing goes off, and pain radiates up my side.

My legs give out from under me, and I hit the ground, seeing Amanda's wide fear-filled eyes as she turns around to look at me. "Run!" I scream, and her eyes widen more; then she takes off. I fight through the pain and force myself to get up, then hear another shot and another, not registering the pain. Instead, I'm focused on the sound of the sirens that seem to be getting closer before everything goes dark.

I wake to the sound of beeping. My tired eyes open slowly and see nothing familiar as I look around the sparsely decorated room. I attempt to sit up, but the pain in my side and back makes it almost impossible to move; then the weight of a heavy hand presses against my shoulder, and I meet Calvin's worry-filled gaze.

"Don't move, baby," he says gruffly, pressing his lips to my forehead as he reaches over me. "Are you in pain?" I nod, and his expression softens. "I'm sorry," he whispers; then, before I can tell him that it's not his fault, darkness creeps over me, and I fall asleep once more.

"She's our daughter; you can't keep us from her!" I hear my father shout, and I blink my eyes open at a low rumbled response I can't make out and the sound of shuffling. I start to sit up to see what's going on, then stop when a hand takes hold of mine. I turn my head to the side. I see Edie and watch her eyes fill with relief as they lock on mine.

"Welcome back, honey."

Welcome back? I close my eyes, and everything that happened flashes through my mind like a bolt of lightning. Tears clog my throat, and I breathe through my nose, trying to get my emotions under control. "Calvin." I whimper his name, needing him more than I need my next breath.

A hand smooths the hair back from my face, lips touch my forehead, and warmth fills my senses as Calvin whispers, "I'm right here, baby."

He's here, right here, with me, where he's supposed to be. I lift my hands, lock my arms around his strong shoulders, and hold on to him, vowing to never let him go. "Sandy."

"She's gone; she can't hurt you."

"Gone?"

"Dead," Calvin whispers, and the tears I've been trying to hold back slip from between my lashes while pain radiates through my chest. I know she wasn't a good person, but she was unwell, and the human part of me hates that she died before she could get help.

"Shhhh." He pulls back, and I blink my eyes open as he swipes the tears from my cheeks. "I love you." He rests his forehead to mine.

"I love you too," I say as my eyelids start to grow heavy.

"Sleep, baby. When you wake back up, we'll start our forever."

Before I can tell him I'm looking forward to that, darkness takes me, but I fall back to sleep with a smile.

Suggestion 15

FOREVER ISN'T LONG ENOUGH

CALVIN

I stare at the ceiling and focus on Anna: the weight of her against my side, the warmth of her naked body curled into mine, and the sound of her breathing. Even with her centering me, bringing me back to reality, my mind keeps replaying what happened, what could have happened. It's been over two months since the worst day of my life, and in that time, Anna has healed almost completely, but that doesn't mean my mind has. When I read Sandy's note, I knew immediately that she was going to go after Anna, but I wasn't able to protect the woman I love. The doctors who performed emergency surgery on Anna said it was a miracle that no major arteries or organs were hit, considering Sandy shot her three times, twice at close range, before the officer who arrived on the scene took Sandy's life on my front lawn.

As a detective, I failed. I didn't notice Sandy's obsession with me. Something I should have recognized if I had been paying attention. Looking back, I remember all the times she happened to show up at different locations where I'd be; seeing her drive by my house, even though she didn't live in my neighborhood; as well as a hundred other little signs. I shouldn't have brushed her off as another dead end just because I thought I knew her. If I had done more, if I had dug deeper, I might have been able to prevent her from hurting anyone else, and almost taking away the most important thing in my life.

I'm angry that her life ended before I could question her. I hate that no one will ever understand how she could have taken three lives so easily. I should feel relieved she's gone, that she can't harm anyone else, but the detective in me hates that she will never face a jury and answer for the crimes she committed. I hate even more that I was the cause of all of it.

"You need to sleep," Anna whispers into the dark, and I dip my chin down toward her, wondering how I didn't notice she was awake when these days my body is completely tuned in to hers. I know when she walks into a room I'm in or when she leaves; I know what her mood is, just by her tone; and I can tell if something is on her mind just by observing her.

"I'm okay." I kiss her forehead, beyond grateful that I can, when there were hours while she was in surgery when I wondered how I would survive if she didn't.

"You say that, but I know you aren't. You haven't been sleeping much the last few weeks since I've been home." She gets up on an elbow and places her face close to mine. "Do you want to talk about whatever it is that's on your mind?"

"No," I say, knowing I never want her to be up thinking about the shit that plagues me in the dark.

"I'm okay—I'm here, and I'm not going anywhere." Her voice is soft as she places her hand on my chest.

"I know, baby. I just need time to forget how close I came to losing you."

Without a word, she slides her hand down my stomach to cup me through my boxers. "Maybe I need to remind you that you didn't lose me and that we are both alive." She straddles my thighs, then slides over me, and the heat of her pussy brushes my skin, making me harder than I already was. When she's kneeling between my legs, she moves her hand up my stomach, and my muscles tighten in anticipation.

"What are you doing, baby?"

"Going to help you remember." She kisses my stomach, then pulls the elastic of my boxers down, and I lift my hips to help her.

My cock springs free, and she wraps her hand around the base, then slides it up to the tip slowly. "Don't tease me, baby," I growl, weaving my fingers into the hair at the side of her head. I see her smile before she licks the head, making my hips jerk in response. "Anna."

"Calvin." She places me against her tongue, then takes me into her mouth, using suction as she deep-throats me.

"Jesus." My head falls back to the pillow, and my eyes squeeze shut.

"You okay, Detective Miller?" There's a hint of a smile in her voice as she uses her hand, twisting and pulling hard as she jerks me off.

"Don't play with me, Anna," I hiss.

"What are you going to do?" she asks, then takes me fully into her mouth once more, so deep that I hit the back of her throat. I feel her shift as she sucks me off, and when I lose her hand, I know she's touching herself. I flip on the lamp, not wanting to miss a moment.

"Come here," I order, wanting her taste, and she shakes her head, never faltering in her manipulation of my cock with her hand and mouth. "Are you sinking your fingers into your pussy?" She nods. "I want a taste of that. Give me your fingers," I say, and she hesitates a moment, then brings her hand up, and I take her wrist and suck her fingers into my mouth, making her whimper around my cock. "I want more. Come up here and give it to me."

She releases me from her mouth, keeping her hand moving. "I want to take care of you."

"Then give me what I want," I say, and she crawls up my body to straddle my hips.

I skim my hand up her side and cup her breast.

"I want you inside me." She lowers her face toward mine, and I lean up, taking her mouth in a deep kiss, and then roll her to her back and pull away. "Calvin."

"You want me?"

"Yes."

"I want you too." I circle her neck, then slowly move my hand down between her breasts, over her stomach, and between her legs, listening to her breath escalate. I skim her clit, and her nails dig into my shoulders. "You're so wet, Anna." I thrust two fingers inside her and she moans, pressing her hips down and taking more. I slide my fingers in and out of her slowly and circle her clit with my thumb, listening to her whimper. I lick and nip her throat, then pause to manipulate her breast with my tongue and teeth. When she's on the verge of orgasm, I flip her to her stomach, then wrap my arm around her waist to lift her up so that she's kneeling in front of me. She rests her head back against my shoulder, and her hands cover mine, even as I move up to cup her breast. "I love you," I whisper against the skin of her neck, and she turns to look at me.

"I love you too." She raises her hands up and behind her head to wrap around my neck.

I glide my fingers down her stomach, through the lips of her pussy, and roll over her clit, pressing my hips into her ass, my cock nudging her sex.

"You're so wet." I nip her ear. "Are you ready to come?"

"Yes." She digs her nails into my thighs and rolls her hips back, causing the tip of my cock to slide against her entrance.

"Calvin." She tips her hips back toward me, trying to take more.

"Easy." I lick across her lips, then shove my tongue into her mouth, entering her and feeling her gasp against my tongue.

"Oh God," she whimpers, falling to her hands as I thrust in and out of her. Her pussy convulses around my cock. I cup her ass, fucking into her as she cries out my name.

Needing more from her, I pull out and carefully flip her to her back, then enter her once more before lowering my head and taking her mouth. When I pull away, I slide my fingers into the hair at the side of her head. "You're the best thing that's ever happened to me," I say, watching tears slide down her temple into her hair. "I want to marry you, Anna."

"Calvin." Her hands go to my shoulders, where her nails dig in, and I plant myself deep inside her, locking my eyes on hers.

"Tell me you'll marry me." I'm not afraid to beg, if that's what she needs me to do.

"I'll marry you." She cups my jaw, then lifts up to touch her lips to mine. I kiss her back as her inner walls ripple around me, pulling my orgasm closer to the surface. "You're the best chance I ever took."

"Fuck." I thrust into her three more times, then squeeze my eyes closed and lose myself inside her. Breathing heavily, I lean back to look at her. "How the fuck did I get so lucky?"

"How did I?" she asks with love shining in her eyes.

"You baited me the first time I saw you, Anna, and since then, you've hooked and reeled me in. I'm so fucking lucky you took a chance on me and on us, and I promise you will never regret that decision."

"Are we really going to get married?" she asks quietly, her eyes roaming my face.

I smile, skimming my thumb along the edge of her bottom lip. "We are definitely getting married and having lots of babies," I say, letting her go as I sit up, bringing her with me so I can open the drawer on my side table and find the box I've been keeping there. Once I have hold of it, I take out the simple diamond ring inside, and she laughs as I slide it onto her finger.

"I planned on asking you when I took you fishing next weekend and was going to hook the ring onto the end of your line." I lift her hand and kiss her finger. "I hope this moment is just as memorable."

"Oh God." She wraps her arms around me right before she sobs.

"Why are you crying?" I ask softly, kissing her hair.

"I . . . I'm so . . . so happy." She leans back to look at me. "That's all I wanted. All I wanted was to be happy, and I thought I knew what that would feel like, but I was wrong. What I feel is better than anything I could have imagined. Thank you for helping me find happiness."

"You found it on your own, baby," I tell her, taking hold of her chin. "It was in you."

"I know, but you made it so much better. You make me better, my life better, and I'm so happy I get to spend the rest of my life with you."

"Forever won't be long enough with you, Anna," I say right before I kiss her.

When I pull back, she grabs my face between her palms. "Will you do something for me?"

"Anything."

"Give yourself a break." She leans in, touching her lips to mine. "I know what happened has been plaguing you, but you couldn't have known what was going to happen, and none of it was your fault."

"Baby . . ."

"Please do it for me . . . for our future. Don't let her have any more of you. She doesn't deserve any part of you that should be mine."

Fuck, she's right. "I'll work on it, baby."

"Promise?"

"I promise." She kisses me once more, then curls against my chest. "I love you."

"I love you too." I turn out the light, then hold tight to the woman who was made for me, vowing to keep my promise to her because she's right: she deserves all of me.

Epilogue

ANNA

With my eyes closed, I listen to the sound of water lapping the shore and the sweet sound of my husband's and daughter's laughter as they play a few feet away in the sand. It's been five years since I left my life behind in Chicago, having no idea if I was doing the right thing but just hoping beyond hope that I was. Obviously things worked out just how they were supposed to and better than I ever imagined they would. Since I took that leap of faith, I've made some really great friends, met the man of my dreams, had a baby girl, and am now pregnant with a little boy. My life is filled with love, happiness, great friendships, and, thankfully, very little drama.

I signed every share of the company over to my father, thinking that when I did, I wouldn't hear from him or my mom again. Surprisingly, that wasn't the case. Not that we're close, but we do talk on occasion, and they check in on their granddaughter, Kennedy, and send her cards and presents on holidays and her birthdays. I'm still very close with Edie, who Kennedy calls MawMaw, and still keep my weekly visits with her, Pearl, and Dixie to gossip or go play bingo. But normally Edie can be found at my house, spending time with "her girls."

"Mommy!" I lean up on my elbow to look at my baby, who's growing bigger by the day, and smile when she walks toward me. "Can we go to the bakery on the way home and get cupcakes?"

"I think we can do that." Her smile looks just like her dad's. Much to Calvin's disappointment, she didn't get my hair or eye color but got his dark hair and blue eyes, which I love.

"Babe, when we go to the shop, you're not working," Calvin says, and I look at him, narrowing my eyes slightly.

"I never said I was."

"I know you didn't, but I know you." I want to roll my eyes, but he's right. Even when I'm not supposed to be working at the bakery I'm working at the bakery, but that's because two years ago, Chrissie offered me the opportunity to become coowner, and I took it. I love that my job never feels like work; it just feels like I'm spending time doing something fun with people I like hanging out with.

"I won't work," I say when he doesn't drop the look he's giving me.

"I love you." The intensity in his expression tells me just how much.

"I know." I pull in a breath and let it out slowly, looking between the two people who mean more to me than anything else in the world . . . that is, until our son joins us in a few months. As he moves around in my belly, I wonder if one person should ever be this happy, then think it doesn't matter, because that's just the way it is.

Acknowledgments

First, I have to give thanks to God, because without him, none of this would have been possible. Second, I want to thank my husband. I love you now and always—thank you for believing in me, even when I don't always believe in myself. To my beautiful son, you bring such joy into my life, and I'm so honored to be your mom. To my sister, my mom, and my family and friends, every single day I'm grateful for the love and happiness you bring into my life.

To every blogger and reader, thank you for taking the time to read and share my books. There will never be enough ink in the world to acknowledge you all, but I will forever be grateful to each and every one of you.

Like thousands of authors before me, I started this writing journey after I fell in love with reading. I wanted to give people a place to escape to where the stories were funny, sweet, and hot and left them feeling good. I've loved sharing my stories with you all, loved that I've helped people escape the real world, even for a moment.

I started writing for me and will continue writing for you.

XOXO,

Aurora

About the Author

Aurora Rose Reynolds is a *New York Times* and *USA Today* bestselling author whose wildly popular series include Until, Until Him, Until Her, and Underground Kings. Her writing career started as an attempt to get the outrageous alpha men in her head to leave her alone and has blossomed into an opportunity to share her stories with readers all over the world.

To stay up to date on what's happening, join the Alpha Mailing List: https://bit.ly/2GXYsVS. To order signed books, go to https://AuroraRoseReynolds.com. You can reach Reynolds via email at auroraroser@gmail.com and follow her on Instagram (@Auroraroser), Facebook (AuthorAuroraRoseReynolds), and Twitter (@Auroraroser).